To Re

from

Lammergeier
and other stories

Lammergeier
and other stories

John Bolland

© John Bolland, 2023

Published by W. J. Bolland

A CIP catalogue record for this book is available from the British Library.

ISBN 978-1-3999-6412-8

Book layout and cover design by Clare Brayshaw

Cover image 44895437 © Dan Talson | Dreamstime.com

Prepared and printed by:

York Publishing Services Ltd
64 Hallfield Road
Layerthorpe
York YO31 7ZQ

Tel: 01904 431213

Website: www.yps-publishing.co.uk

Contents

Lammergeier

'In its mountain habitat the Lammergeier is unmistakable, with its long narrow wings and wedge-shaped tail, the ochre or deep red of the head and neck a result of its habit of rubbing feathers with pigmented sand.... It can bite through bones the size of a lamb's femur and may carry a bone too large to be swallowed to a height of fifty to a hundred metres, dropping it on the rocks below, smashing it into smaller pieces to expose the marrow....'

Tim glanced from his copy of *European Birds* to the soft sunlit bed of white cloud he could see through the plane's window. Hard to imagine the unforgiving peaks and crags of the Pyrenees a few thousand feet below. The Lammergeier was next on the list of birds he most wanted to see. After the Black Woodpecker in the Carpathians and the Californian Condor, tracked down with the help of local guides, he was on the trail of number three in the Picos Mountains of Northern Spain. 'A preferred prey is the tortoise, carried to a great height and dropped to crack open the nutritious inside. According to legend the Greek playwright Aeschylus was killed when a tortoise was dropped on his bald head by an eagle, which may have mistaken it for a large stone. It is likely that a Lammergeier was responsible....'

'What a tragedy,' Tim giggled, as his lunchtime gin and tonic began to have its effect. A little later he was in a troubled dream-laden sleep: – he was on a bed of cotton wool, soft, warm and sustaining like the Jacuzzi in a luxury spa; a sudden sharp pain in his right thigh, a confusion of wings, a red beak; then swept up to heaven like Elijah, only to be released by what were now disconcertingly human red lips, and down, down till his body shattered into pieces on a stone ledge by the entrance to a cave. As happens in dreams, he began desperately to gather up the pieces, trying to put them together again.

Tim awoke to find the pointed foot of his telescope tripod digging into his thigh. He moved it to one side and once more checked on the telescope in the overhead locker; his new telescope, the Swarovski Modular Digiscope, capable of high definition telephoto pictures and many other technical feats he would never fully understand. From the cabin window he could see the grey waters of the Bay of Biscay as the plane turned to make its descent into Santander. Coming through Arrivals, he saw a placard with his name, Timothy Torbert, and next to it the smiling face of his guide and host, Xavi.

After a drive of an hour or so they reached Panes in the foothills of the Picos, and stopped at a hotel by the river Deva, where Xavi had arranged a little welcome party with the mayor and some local worthies. Over a glass of wine and some tapas, the talk turned from Griffon Vultures and Alpine Accentors to politics and the state of the local economy, when Tim's attention was caught by a statuesque female figure standing in an alcove, looking intently at the river. She seemed to be from another era. A delicate mantilla fell from the head, in half profile, and merged with soft coils of black hair and a dress of some dark-patterned silky material. Even in the dim light of the bar, the low bodice, the deep red of the lips above the ivory bosom, the finely arched eyebrows made an arresting image; a Goya, Tim thought, amidst the plastic tablecloths and advertisements for San Miguel. He looked enquiringly to his hosts.

'Ah,' sighed the mayor, '*la dama de los dolores con la voz de un ángel*. If only you heard her Tosca when she toured New York, Vienna, Paris – *fue sublime*.' Tim pressed for more details and learned that Alicia Marquesa came from close by in Llonin, that she was a child prodigy who became a famous soprano, the pride of Panes, until a septic throat damaged her voice and cut short a promising career. She had come back to live on her mother's farmhouse high up in the mountains. 'No Panes man good enough. Sometime I hear her singing when I walk up there, but is not the same, sounds sweet but weaker now.' The mayor brought his tale to an end. As the little group left the hotel, the woman in the mantilla happened to turn and fixed Tim with a penetrating stare. A little flustered, he stumbled out of the door.

A few hours later he was comfortably lodged in a semi-detached farm worker's cottage nestling in the foothills above the Deva. The supper of bean and pork stew and the half bottle of red wine provided by the caretaker had left him drowsy and in reflective mood, wondering what had brought him, alone, to the Picos Mountains. He had entered his career of librarianship expecting Victorian interiors with deep leather armchairs, academic researchers to exchange quotations with, promising young female novelists to find references for. But the academics were surly and uncommunicative and no novelists appeared. When librarianship developed into information

3

management, with digital search engines, desks replaced by computer stations, he felt out of place and out of his depth, and took advantage of a very favourable early retirement scheme. Since then birdwatching had assumed a major role in his life. He could pursue rare and beautiful creatures, and capture them with a lovingly executed sketch or, as now, perhaps, with a high-definition photo. He thought with some excitement of his next quarry, the Lammergeier.

At that moment, a few miles away, Alicia was also completing her preparations for bed. She stood before her mirror removing the layers of make-up from her face and neck and the red lipstick, still a beautiful woman, but the full lips had become a little thinner, the downturn at the corners of her mouth a little more pronounced, the fine creases under her eyes like contour lines on a map. Perfect in early womanhood for roles like Carmen or Tosca, she was now easier to imagine as a striking but gaunt Antigone or Electra – a Papas rather than a Cruz. After her mother's death, she had lived alone in the remote farmhouse, her mountainside eyrie as the townspeople put it, struggling to sustain the decaying family estate and keep control of unruly tenants. Rural Spain was not accustomed to an independent woman in a position of power. There were men who wanted to marry her, men like Luis Fonseca, the local accountant, but how could she, Alicia Marquesa, bury herself in a provincial town, the wife of some boring petit bourgeois? She remembered her debut as Lucia di Lammermoor, the adulation of the crowds, the rave reviews and the sequence of lovers. She looked at the figure in the mirror, unfulfilled, ageing, and she softly sang some of her favourite lines as Lucia driven mad by love. Finally, she made her way to her bed. For some reason she found her thoughts returning to the pale, gawky foreigner she had seen at the Casa Cortina.

Tim had set his alarm for an early start the next morning, and after porridge, *pan rustico* and coffee, he was outside the cottage, waiting for Xavi. A hot day was expected and he was wearing the gilet, khaki shirt and shorts he had bought from the local Barbour outlet, a lightweight airflo Tilly hat on his head for the sun. The gleaming black of the Swarovski rose up behind his head, safe in its back pack. He could hear sounds of preparation from the adjoining cottage, and three men soon appeared. He was taken aback to find that they were kitted out exactly like him, though the fabric was a little more worn, and the Swarovskis on their backs were clearly higher-end than his. They were a family of three generations of birdwatchers, the Arkwrights from Birmingham, and soon fell into conversation with Tim. The little huddle could have been a heavily armed special ops unit being briefed for a sortie in the steaming jungles of Burma.

'All royt?' said the middle Arkwright. 'I'm Ted. That's the ATX 30-75x95 innit?' pointing at the telescope, 'with the DSLR Canon Eos 7D? A royt mint combo.'

'I wouldn't know,' said Tim, ' bit of a technophobe.'

'No probs,' said the youngest, Phil. 'I'll give you a hand. Just connect scope to't Canon with the adaptor, like. I'll set up default link to Twitcherfeed, and all you've to do with your shot is press this button. Kerboom! It's up there shared with Chris Packham and Bill Oddie. Let's have scope and yer phone.'

After some pushing of widgets on Tim's scope and mobile, they were ready to test the system on the first bird they saw. He pressed the shutter button. Click. Minutes later, sure enough, a buzz on his mobile. His first tweet.

'Well done, Tim, *Turdus Merula*, the common or garden blackbird. Keep up the good work! a.nowell@ ebird.'

'Welcome to the world of digiscoping,' said Mervyn, and Tim beamed, gratified at the ease with which he seemed to have mastered the technology.

At that moment Xavi arrived. A busy little blackbird himself, he jumped out of the car, dived into the boot for the picnic lunches, distributed them to his little brood, packed telescopes and tripods, and hustled them all into the Seat.

'Will we see any Golden Eagles?' asked Phil.

'We will hav'em,' said Xavi, his head on one side nodding furiously.

'Any chance of Wallcreepers?' asked Phil's father.

'We will hav'em.'

'I trust we will have the Lammergeier too,' said Tim.

'We will hav'em,' more hesitantly.

And Xavi delivered.

Hiding in scrub on a hillside the four birders look across a ravine to a dark smudge on the cliffs opposite. Telescopes reveal a small cave, a hint of movement. An hour's wait and then a plaintiff, puppy like yelping when the golden eagle senses the arrival of her mate. A pale brown shape glides down to the cave, a dead baby chamois in its talons. A frenzy of squealing as the prey is delivered to mother and nestling. Click. The photo is taken and sent to Twitcherfeed. Up the *teleférico* at Fuente De, through the clouds and into the craggy grey peaks. Close-ups of Alpine choughs floating above the white blanket. Click. Along the shallow canyon between sheer rock-faces. Grandfather Mervyn tries out his bird call app imitating the distressed cries of a Snow Finch. A male appears, circles menacingly and dives towards Mervyn, searching for its mate. Click. Up into the snowline where the canyon narrows and the air sharpens. News of Wallcreepers sighted on a cliff. Ploughing through deep snow for a view, regretting shorts. Midge-like specks flit across the rock face, transformed through the scope into an exquisite miniature Audubon print. Long thin beak, pale grey head shading into charcoal, a splash of red on the shoulder, black wings barred with white. The Wallcreeper. Click.

On the third evening the group met for a debriefing at a taberna outside Llonin. The Arkwrights were beginning to tot up and compare their lists of sightings, but Tim was more philosophical, reflecting on the forces of nature that drove the eagle to hunt food for its young and the little Snow Finch to risk its life to rescue its mate. For the first time in his life, he had met with something beyond the orbit of the Norwich City Library. True, he had been witness to the odd foot stamped in anger over a fine for an overdue book, even to occasional raised voices, but creatures driven by instinct and impulse... and his thoughts turned again to the *dama de los dolores*. What passions smouldered behind that intense stare? A buzz in his pocket announced yet another tweet, 'Love the Wallcreeper mate. chris@springwatch.' His birdshots were trending on Twitcherfeed, three hundred hits to date.

There was, of course, a species absent from their lists, the Lammergeier. Xavi decided that their chances would be improved if they split the group, three going to the Cares Gorge with him, while Tim would be left at a suspected nest on the mountainsides above Llonin. It was important for Tim to be on site before dawn, as the Lammergeier would then leave the nest to patrol its vast territory in search of prey. Preparing for bed that night, Tim felt an unfamiliar ache of anticipation in the pit of his stomach.

Alicia had less to look forward to that night. It had been rent day on the family estate, and the sullen faces of her tenant farmers betrayed a growing anger. Why should they sacrifice precious funds to support a childless single woman? Why should they tolerate cottages, fences and farm tracks in a state of neglect? There would soon be open resistance. She needed funds to maintain the estate. She needed a man to fight her battles, even a man like Luis Fonseca. Fonseca, *Fuente Seca*, dry well, perfect summary of a future life with that banal petit-bourgeois, a life collecting pottery and *cristaleria*, preparing genteel soirees for his clients. She looked again at the offer of marriage she had received that morning. Still, Fonseca it would have to be. She would see him tomorrow.

The next morning Tim is positioned by Xavi at the nest site before dawn. He sets up his tripod and scope looking over a farmhouse below him towards the cliffs where the nest is not yet visible. Darkness thins. A rim of sun appears on the horizon. He can see the nest. The orange disc clears the horizon, bathing in gold the walls and curtained windows of the farmhouse below. He focuses his scope on the nest in the cliffs. Suddenly a curtain in one of the farmhouse windows twitches and is drawn. A shock of surprise and his hands jerk the tripod and scope. Click. In some confusion, Tim gathers up his gear and scrambles down the mountainside through the scrub. He pauses when he hears singing in the distance: '*Edgardo! io ti son resa. Edgardo! Ah! Edgardo, mio! Si, ti son resa!*' A beautiful voice, though frail and a little unsteady in the higher registers. Finally he reaches the Llonin road. In mounting panic, he looks at the little screen above his telescope. He has a high resolution image of a woman in a nightdress looking out of her bedroom window. 'Sent' he reads. Right now it is hurtling through the World Wide Web.

Repercussions soon followed. The digital image had gone viral and the tweets flooded in:

'Nice one Tim, but not one for Springwatch eh? chris@ springwatch.'

'Please give map co-ordinates. ken@ebird.'

'I have to inform you that your membership of Norfolk Wildlife Trust has been suspended in view of activities not in keeping with the NWT mission. robingannet@cley-by-sea.'

The next day Tim was visited by the mayor who had brought the town's lawyer to underline the gravity of the situation. Panes was a remote, rural town, but its inhabitants were net savvy, and enlarged prints of Alicia were already circulating in the bars and tabernas. She was clothed, of course, but the nightdress was sufficiently negligee for the photo to be thought provocative, and Luis Fonseca, considering his position in the town, had already announced he was withdrawing his proposal of marriage. Furthermore, there was the possibility of criminal proceedings, as the lawyer explained.

'Since the time of Franco, sir, we in Spain have been very protective of women's honour. We do not tolerate violence, any form of violence, to the women. May I refer you to Article 180 of the Criminal Code, where it specifies a prison sentence of five to ten years (taking out some sheets of paper) 1. When violence or intimidation towards women is of a particularly degrading or humiliating nature. 2. When the victim is vulnerable due to circumstances. 3. When in order to execute the offence, the offender has availed himself of a superiority due to being in an ascendant position. I am afraid, sir, all these conditions seem to have been met in your case. The outlook is extremely grave. All rests on whether Doña Marquesa chooses to make a formal complaint.'

Alicia was also coming to terms with her situation. It had been her custom on waking to throw open the bedroom window to receive the morning sun on her body and to sing an *aubade*. On the fateful day she had done so as usual, barely noticing some movement on the slopes opposite, but over the next hours her predicament was brought home to her – a letter from Fonseca withdrawing his proposal of marriage, and then an enlarged print of herself, defaced with obscene additions, pushed under her door. She went into Panes to investigate and was met with sneers or scornful laughter. She had lost caste in the town. What did the future hold for her now?

The next day the Mayor paid her a visit. An English birdwatcher sent to prison for five years would be bad news for a local economy reliant on tourism, and to salvage the situation he hoped to encourage a relationship between offender and victim. To this end he had done some investigation into Tim's background, and began to outline a glowing character reference for him, when Alicia interrupted.

'Who is this Teemothy...?'

'Torbert! Timothy Torbert!

'This man he is young?'

'Yes, he is very young for retired English gentleman.'

'He is wealthy?'

'Yes, he has index-linked pension. Plus half a lump sum.'

'Teemothy Torrbert, *muy distinguido*, yes? I am going to have him!'

In the weeks that followed, an acquaintance between Tim and Alicia developed into friendship, and then into something more. She found his Barbour gilet '*muy elegante*' and his high-pitched English tones '*reconfortante*' after the basses and baritones of the Latin lovers of her youth. She liked to hear him talk about the big skies of Norfolk, the slow progress of sails across a Broads horizon, the whispering reeds, the booming of the bittern, the courtship of the great crested grebe. She liked to hear him recite his favourite passages, from Prufrock, La Belle Dame.... Of an evening, in the fastness of her mountainside home, she, on her part, would reprise for Tim her favourite operatic roles, including *Lucia di Lammermoor*, helpfully translated into English. Tim had always been taken with the *dama de los dolores*, and hearing her 'Edgardo! I surrender to you, oh my Edgardo! ...' awakened, as he put it, certain importunate, primordial drives within himself. He was enthralled, enraptured by the emotional power her voice still carried. Quite smitten. The prospect of prison also heightened the ardour with which he pursued her hand. His proposal was accepted and their betrothal sealed with a crushing embrace. The date of the wedding was decided for late summer. There was no more talk of violence and intimidation. His one regret was his failure to 'have' the Lammergeier.

By late summer in Asturias the chilling Atlantic winds have abated and the temperature can rise into the 80s. It had been a hot August day for the wedding but it was cool by the evening when guests gathered at a long table outside Alicia's farmhouse to enjoy the *banquete de la boda*. The Mayor was guest of honour; some of Alicia's kinsmen had travelled from distant estates; her tenants were now reconciled and soon tucking into the paella, happy with the promise of a big cash injection into the estate; Tim was represented by Xavi, head to one side, nodding furiously at the Arkwrights, who had made the journey from Birmingham to support their fellow birder. The bride and groom had been circulating with presents for the guests and the Mayor was laughing at something whispered to him by the bride, when Mervyn noticed a huge bird high in the sky. Long narrow pointed wings, long wedge-shaped tail, diagnostic. 'Lammergeier!' he yelled. 'Get bloody telescope!' Faces at the table looked up and watched the magnificent bird, the slow, effortless soaring, gradually getting lower and lower until she glided gracefully into her nest. She seemed to be carrying something in her talons. The crushed thigh bone of a lamb? The broken body of a tortoise?

A Gentle Knight[1]

The winter of nineteen sixty-five had been brutally cold in Norwich, and to save shillings on our gas fire we got into the habit of spending Saturday afternoons in Elm Hill, in a second-hand bookshop which was always generously heated by paraffin stoves. That particular afternoon I had taken down an old edition of Spenser's *Faerie Queen* and was turning over its fragile pages, entranced by illustrations of knights and monsters.

'Not to everyone's taste, Spenser,' said a deep voice behind me, 'but such a wonderful opening. "A gentle knight was pricking on the plaine/Ycladd in mightie armes and silver shield".' The voice belonged to a tall, bearded man of that indeterminate age above fifty. He wore a heavy black woollen coat that seemed to reach down to his ankles, and his neck was encircled several times by a grey scarf. 'Willis Feast, nice to meet you,' he said, and his face and eyes expressed such a genuine, lively interest in us, poor, insignificant, woefully ignorant students as we were, barely out of our teens, that Debbie and I took to him immediately.

Introductions complete, it seemed that Willis Feast was rector of a country parish some twelve miles from

---

1 This story is a re-imagining of actual events and incidents

Norwich. 'Look, you must come to tea tomorrow at the rectory,' he said. 'My wife and family would be delighted to meet you and we will be able to have a jolly good literary talk.' With that he sketched out directions to Booton rectory on the back of one of the shop's catalogues.

Booton is only twelve miles from Norwich, but the next afternoon the temperature was well below zero and we arrived on my scooter at Willis Feast's house too frozen to notice the impressive church or the neo-Jacobean grandeur of the rectory itself behind its curtain of mature trees. With helmets, gloves, and overcoats removed, we were ushered into a room with a blazing fire and introduced to Feast's wife, who immediately pointed out how cold Debbie must be and took her to a fireside seat. In the middle of the room a table was spread with varieties of sandwiches, scones with a selection of jams, and cakes, Victoria sponge, Dundee, Battenburg. I made my choice while Mrs. Feast filled a plate for Debbie. To one side of the fireplace shelves full of books rose up to the high ceiling. We had barely taken a sip of tea when the Reverend Feast began to talk of his fondness for modern poetry, picking out volumes from the shelves and reading passages. As his wife plied us with more tea and cakes, we were quizzed on our favourite poets and novelists and he treated our callow judgements with genuine interest and respect. All the while, from the recesses of the house could be heard children's and adults' voices. There was clearly not just a family but a community living in the rectory who would partake of the spread on the table in due course. As the light faded outside, we said we should make the return trip to Norwich, and Mrs. Feast insisted on lending Debbie a pair of thick leather knee-length boots for the cold, which she promised to return by post.

Now, in two thousand and sixteen, I had been drawn back to Booton, alone. I stood near the rectory, hidden by a tall holly hedge and trees in summer foliage. I could still recall in vivid detail that first meeting and the hospitable tea we enjoyed on a freezing winter's day, but I knew so much more now, about Booton rectory and its church. I knew that the kindly rector's wife who had served us tea had once smacked a woman, smacked her in the very room, probably, where we had enjoyed buttered scones with jam and Victoria sponge cake.

In July 1940, a report appeared in a local Norfolk newspaper: 'Mrs. Ella Gwendolen Tilden Smith, of Holt, was fined for being drunk and disorderly on the highway at Holt... Police Constable Haverson stated defendant was unsteady on her feet, her appearance was dishevelled and her breath smelled of spirits.' Evidently Mrs. Tilden Smith had shouted abuse at the English race, saying that 'they were a bloody mean and dirty lot.' In mitigation it was pointed out that the disorderly conduct had only arisen when a bucket of cold water was thrown over the accused and that she had been in a distressed state due to lack of news of her daughter in recently invaded Holland.

The incident in Holt was one of several Mrs. Tilden Smith had been involved in since she joined her husband in Norfolk on his appointment as an administrative officer in the RAF. It was to culminate some time later in a scene in a pub in Thorpe, an area of Norwich, where, irritated by some offensive drinkers, she rose and shouted 'Heil Hitler!', provocative to say the least at a time when the Lutwaffe had begun its bombing of Norwich. Captain Tilden Smith had to be removed from his post in Norfolk as a security risk and discreetly sent to Bristol.

Originally from Dominica, Mrs. Tilden Smith's feelings of racial insecurity were heightened by war-time paranoia, as a result of which people regarded a woman who looked and spoke differently as a possible enemy alien. Fuelled by gin, imagined slights would flare up into full-scale rows, even violence, necessitating moves from village to village, until she and her husband found themselves in digs in Norwich. By now Mrs. Tilden Smith was drinking heavily and on the verge of a nervous breakdown. She was seeing a psychiatrist, a Doctor Rose in Norwich.

Mrs. Tilden Smith was of course Jean Rhys, by then the writer of five acclaimed novels and considered by some to be the greatest stylist of the Twentieth Century. In 1941, in the middle of the first air raids on Norwich, a friend, recognising her desperate situation and acquainted with the idealism and kindness of Willis Feast, appealed to him to save the struggling novelist by taking her to Booton. He agreed and her salvation became his quest.

Feast arrived at Rhys's flat in the Chapelfield area of Norwich with his eldest daughter Barbara, just thirteen at the time. He had been a handsome young man (there is a portrait of him in chalk, broad browed, hint of a smile, by Wyndham Lewis in the Norwich castle collection), and perhaps to avoid any hint of impropriety or just for moral support he felt the need of his daughter's company. Rhys appeared at the door of her flat dressed in Parisian chic of the 1920s, a figure-hugging dark dress with a broad belt, white butterfly collar on the bosom, set off by a beret at a rakish angle. She was fifty years old but still a beautiful woman ('like Claudette Colbert', according to Barbara), with her large pale eyes and arched eyebrows. Feast led her to his old Morris, and the three got in, Rhys remembering no doubt happier times being driven along the coastal roads of Juan les Pins in Ford Madox Ford's Corniche.

Feast held a great respect for Rhys as an important novelist but also as a woman who had suffered much. She was given the best bedroom in the house, overlooking the back garden, and it was made clear that she could join the family for meals or have them delivered to her room if she preferred to be private. On the occasions she joined the family and their friends for dinner, she would look 'very regal' and could be very entertaining, at least to start with, recalling her times in the demi-monde of 20s and 30s Paris.

'Oh I knew all the writers for Ford's *Atlantic Review*, you know, Gertrude Stein, Djuna Barnes, Ezra Pound. Hemingway, not so well, though he was very kind, helped me on with my coat when I was in tears after some barbed comment from Stella and wanted to leave *Les Deux Magots*; not so easy living in a ménage à trois. (Mrs. Feast looking embarrassed, the thirteen year old Barbara interested, the friend Reverend Griffiths disapproving). I was painted, by Royal Academy artists, you know, first Sir Edward Poynter, and then younger, but more fun, Sir William Orpen. He was so kind when I first took off my clothes, called me a nymph and gave me a beautiful blue chiffon dress. In the middle of painting he would suddenly stop, put on a record and dance a Highland fling. But in the provinces here in England they have no respect for the artistic world or high society. They forget I come from a wealthy white Creole plantation family in Dominica and my first lover Lancy, Lancelot Grey Hugh Smith to you, was an English aristocrat. Yes, you provincial English, (looking aggressively at the diners at the table), you regard me as a sad, gin-soaked embarrassment. You are a sexually repressed lot, with your 'respectability', and your deep hatred of women. I am sick of the woman hatred in this country. It's so mean, so stupid and so ugly, that it would be mean and cowardly not to fight back. (Turning for support to Mrs. Feast and Barbara, who looked studiously at their plates, never having considered themselves in this light before; the Reverend Griffiths scoffing). And then when I think of my poor daughter Maryvonne in Holland, at the mercy of those dreadful Boches. I cannot stand it any longer!'

Rhys began to spend more and more time locked in her room. Fits of screaming would be followed by bouts of manic laughter as she remembered incidents of race hatred, the consequence of years of slavery in Dominica. Sometimes, in the middle of the night, she would pace the corridors of the rectory, much like her heroine in *Wide Sargasso Sea*, muttering resentment at the cold, repressed English, re-living terrifying memories from her childhood: 'Look Doudou! In the shadows, see the *loups-garoux*!' 'Black devil! Black devil!'

In early summer, nights in the vicarage could still be cool, and one evening Barbara was sent up with a hot water bottle. Detecting some disrespect in the teenager's tone Rhys turned on her: 'What insolence! You think you are the belle of the village with your summer frocks and freckles. Huh! *Fille mal élevée*! The nuns of my convent school in Roseau would have taught you some manners ....' The next day, all contrition, she gave Barbara a tortoiseshell bangle and Mrs. Feast a favourite black silk dress. 'Ah, the memories. I used to wear it at the Café Royal before a night of pleasure with Lancy.'

'Thank you so much,' said Mrs. Feast, making a mental note she would save it for the Harvest Festival supper.

Reverend Feast was becoming more and more concerned and, in an attempt to draw Rhys out of her seclusion, he offered one evening to take her to lunch and shopping in Norwich. The following morning she appeared downstairs at her most regal, heavily made up and dressed in a dark blue velvet dress and a little blue hat with an ostrich feather. No doubt she was expecting to be taken to the best table in The Royal, but found herself instead being led by Feast to a window table at the Lyons Corner House.

'Are you trying to insult me? Am I so déclassée that it has come to this? A Lyons Corner House?' With that she took one look at the menu, threw it up in the air and rushed out of the restaurant and into the maze of alleys in Norwich market. Eventually Feast found her in the Sir Garnet Wolsey, gin in hand and denouncing the English to an increasingly restive group of farmers who had come in to the city on market day.

As the weather became warmer in late summer, Rhys would take a rug and cushion and sit in the shade of a beech tree in the vicarage garden, enjoying the peaceful English scene and reading Hemingway's *For Whom the Bell Tolls*. Encouraged by these signs of improvement, Feast decided to organise a picnic for her with some clerical friends, a '*déjeuner sur l'herbe*', as he put it. The curates from St. Andrews Holt and St Mary's Reepham were invited, and Feast's friend Eric Griffiths, rector of nearby Brandiston. Rhys took up position under the beech tree, immaculate in a dress that buttoned down the front, the clergymen arranged at her feet. Immaculate, that is, except, the young curates noticed, for three buttons left undone, the dress being too tight. Rhys had become somewhat plump on the Feasts' hospitality. Feast himself was not part of the group, but kept within earshot, performing chores in the garden, ready to intervene at any sign of trouble. The picnic began well, with Rhys discussing Hemingway's *For Whom the Bell Tolls* between bites of egg and cucumber sandwich.

'Wonderful story, but such a banal style – all those nouns, so matter of fact, I long for a vivid metaphor or simile to spark my imagination.' But then, noticing the rapt attention of the curates, Rhys began to be flirtatious, provocative even, and Feast increasingly anxious. 'Of course, there was no shame in Paris being a kept woman as long as the man was of some consequence. They better understand things there, the difference between *une femme entretenue* and *les filles publiques,* the women of the pavement.' The curates were agog, the rector disapproving and Feast desperate to find some excuse to intervene. 'Did I find much pleasure in the act itself? Not as a young woman. They say (looking intently at the curates) that a woman only begins to enjoy *l'amour* when she is in the autumn of her years.'

'Oh, come now, Mrs. Tilden Smith, late summer, late summer,' interjected the curate from St. Andrews.

This was too much. Feast got out his motor mower, one of the earliest models, started the engine and began to mow wildly, getting ever closer to the *déjeuner sur l'herbe.* The picnickers broke up in disarray, and sandwiches, rugs, and *For Whom the Bell Tolls* were taken into the safety of the rectory. The curates were disappointed, but the curate of St Andrews thought he could make something of the afternoon for his Sunday sermon: 'Wherefore I say unto thee, Her sins, which are many are forgiven, for she loved much.'

Rhys's rally in the summer did not last. By autumn, she was drinking heavily, isolating herself in her room, unable to write, and quick to take offence when she did see someone. Willis Feast, steadfast in his mission, racked his brains. There was flower arranging, of course. Rhys initially seemed receptive to the idea, but when she saw him enter the drawing room with an armful of white rhododendrons, she lost all restraint.

'Ah, the English death flowers,' she yelled, 'with their neat pale heads. Are you wanting my death? Give me the reds and pinks of my childhood, and their wild shapes, the octopus orchid, coralita, hibiscus and flamboyant, then I can create something.'

Her paranoia was out of control, and especially directed at the rector of Brandiston, whom she suspected, rightly, of disapproving of her. It was heading to a crisis and Feast held a meeting in the drawing room with his wife and the rector to discuss what to do.

Suddenly, unexpectedly, Rhys burst in and, noticing the rector of Brandiston, shouted: 'I see the hatred in your eyes. I know you wish me dead, you and your womenfolk. I know they want to stab me with their knitting needles, and you, you wish to see me locked up. But you will not succeed.' With that she rushed to the door leading to the garden. Worried about the harm she might do herself, Feast ran after her. Rhys turned on him: 'Why are you always spying on me, you... you English clergyman!' Feast put a hand on her arm to soothe her, but she flicked it away and began to scream. Hearing the noise, two Feast daughters entered the room. Rhys continued to scream. The children were terrified. At that point Mrs. Feast took over. She began to slap Rhys, until, finally, the screaming stopped. Soon after the incident there was a pause in the bombing of Norwich and Rhys returned to her digs in

Chapelfield, to the relief of most members of the family and their friends.

As I stood by the drive into the rectory, I wondered what had gone wrong. It seemed so noble, the quest to save this brilliant, vital, but desperately insecure writer. And yet, after all, Rhys survived. She went on to write her greatest novel, *Wide Sargasso Sea,* in 1966, and who is to say her months at Booton did not provide essential respite, that the ministrations of its rector did not see her through a crisis that might have destroyed her. This brought me back to the reason for my return to the rectory. I had heard recently of Debbie's death, and being in Norwich for an alumni reunion, I decided to go back to the place where we had spent an enjoyable afternoon together. I remembered Debbie's interest in Willis Feast's anecdotes and the care with which she wrapped up Mrs. Feast's boots to return them to her the next day. It was not long after that we parted. I had begun to spend more and more time in the library, determined to get a good degree, and reluctant to let personal time interfere with my ambitions. On the whole I had succeeded in academia, my rise in seniority unimpeded by emotional entanglements. Debbie did not pursue a career. Soon after graduation, she met and married a clergyman, and spent most of her life in a parish in Hampshire, attending to the duties of a vicar's wife and bringing up her five children. All this from *Alumni News.* I found the information comforting.

It remained to find the grave of Willis Feast and to pay my respects. I walked around the side of St. Michael's to the graveyard. There, near the church wall under a purple lilac in bloom, I found the grave of Elisabeth, his wife, but for Feast himself I could find no memorial in the overgrown churchyard. I could see a young man with a notebook in his hand, also searching. After a while our searches brought us near one another.

'Looking for someone?' he said, somewhat aggressively.

'Yes', I replied, 'the Reverend Feast.'

'Really!' he said 'So am I! But I got here first.'

Astounded, I was trying to make sense of his words when he showed me his notebook. I read, 'Geocache description. Church Micro 3195. The co-ordinates will take you to a resting place for Willis Feast and to find this you will need to fill in the missing answers to NOB5245.4AB from:- In memory of Willis Feast, rector of this parish STUV-WXYZ where A=V, B=Y, C=U-Z and D=Z. You are looking for a blue-topped container slightly bigger than a film container. Additional hint, decrypted: Where Victoria's feet lie.' The young man sat on a tombstone and after some calculations he walked decisively to a grave in the corner of the churchyard: 'In memory of Willis Feast....' A quick search at the bottom of the tombstone, and there it was, the blue-topped container. He took a photograph of me holding the container in front of the tombstone.

'I must be off to a church in Suffolk,' he said. 'I need to find four more geocaches if I'm going to win this month's SAD prize.' I wished him good fortune on his quest and stood there many minutes looking at the memorial to Willis Feast, pleased that our reunion would be forever recorded on a geocacher's app.

The Man in the Tunnel

'It's a man crush thing. Yes, definitely, he's got a crush on you.' Tom reddened, shaking his head at his wife, but pleased to be, at the age of eighty, the object of anyone's infatuation. 'Clutching his leg like that in the tunnel, moaning in pain. What a performance. He knows you used to be a doctor, saw his chance.'

'But it could be serious, Sue. I had to wait until the ambulance was on its way.'

'So here we are, late for Kate and Martin's supper. And you with your condition. Honestly, it's been one excuse after another ever since he returned the scarf you dropped. As if you would have done it deliberately.'

'It's like the scene in that film… *Enduring Love* wasn't it?' said Martin. 'Two men exchange looks while trying to stop a hot air balloon being blown away. One of them thinks it's the start of a relationship and begins stalking the other. It didn't end well, Tom.'

'Misreading objects and gestures for signals,' said Kate, leading her guests to the table. 'You'd better be extra careful with the housework Sue. No hanging sheets out of your window to air. Come on, food's getting cold, let's eat.'

Earlier that evening the short walk to their friends' house had taken Tom and Sue Steward through an underpass full of street art. A brightly lit, comic strip world, its air heavy with the fumes from spray cans, it had provided a break from the wet November night. Leaning against a wall was a man in his fifties with long grey hair, dressed in a khaki coat and brown trousers. It was the man Tom had come to know as Miles. When he sank to the ground clutching his leg and groaning, performance or not, it had been impossible to leave him there. Sue would have to go on to their friends while Tom helped him to his home.

Miles' flat was a few yards from the tunnel, part of a modern block set lower than the street, and directly opposite, higher up the slope, was the terrace of Georgian houses where Tom and Sue lived. With Miles comfortable in an armchair Tom began an examination. He lifted a trouser leg to check for redness and swelling. He pressed the groin area gently for signs of tenderness at the femoral vein. Miles moaned softly. The evidence for thrombosis was inconclusive and Tom decided to phone for an ambulance. While they waited, he took stock of the room: on the floor a foil container with the remains of a curry, bits of naan; socks and underpants thrown on an armchair; on a table a half-drunk glass of wine; books, mostly historical works, stacked on the shelves in untidy piles; over everything a smoke-filled fug. Tom got up to look at the framed photographs on a wall: Miles in a gown clutching his degree, a staff photo with Miles in a row of teachers. Puzzled, he turned to the whimpering figure slumped in a chair. The long damp hair clung to the face, obscuring what Tom could now see were fine features, a tall forehead and delicately shaped mouth.

As they waited, the two of them looked out of the big window, filmy with dust. Above the level of the street they could see the gable ends of Tom's house lit up by the street lamp.

'How long have you lived there?' asked Miles.

'Why, it must be fifty years.'

'Not like the here-today-and-gone-tomorrow people who live in this block... how old is the house, early Georgian?'

'Yes, that's right,' said Tom, surprised.

A pause. 'Must be really interesting inside,' said Miles, looking into Tom's face. At that moment the phone rang. The ambulance was on its way, and, with help at hand, Tom felt able to leave.

From his chair Miles watched Tom climb up the steps to the street. He rose, picked up the phone and dialled 999. He was feeling much better, he told the call handler, and wouldn't be needing the ambulance. He returned to his chair, a smile on his face.

A few weeks later, there was a small gathering at Tom and Sue's to celebrate his eighty-first birthday. The large entrance hall had for some time been turned into a little family museum with paintings and photographs, pieces of antique furniture, professional and academic trophies. Tom was standing with Kate and Martin before the portrait of an ancestor. The doorbell rang. It was Miles. After introductions they all turned to look at the painting, the figure of a man in a black doublet covered in a huge white collar. Kate turned to Tom, smiling, 'I can see the family resemblance....'

'I believe that's a painting of Augustine Steward,' Miles interrupted. 'Your ancestor took a decisive part during Kett's rebellion, you know.' The others looked at him in astonishment.

'So you're the man in the tunnel,' said Kate, winking at Martin. Miles blushed, muttered an excuse and moved away to look at the other objects and paintings in the room. 'A bit social phobic, your friend Miles?' said Kate turning to Tom. Some minutes later Tom noticed Miles slipping out of the front door.

Tom found Miles' appearance at his party troubling. He had left no invitation at his flat. Seeing guests arrive at the house opposite, Miles must have decided to take his chance. There had been the incident in the underpass and here was another intrusion into Tom's life. After a few hours of restless sleep, he woke with a start. It was two in the morning. Wondering what had disturbed him, he made his way downstairs to the entrance hall. In the dark he could make out a figure sitting on one of the chairs. He switched on the light. It was Miles.

'You left your spare key in that bowl,' he said, pointing at a table. 'I just love sitting here. I hope you don't mind.' With that he got up, dropped the key in the bowl and walked out of the house. Following him to the front door, Tom watched him cross the road, his tall shape silhouetted against the bright lights of the tunnel. What had brought Miles out at two in the morning? he wondered. The chance to sit on an antique chair?

Tom's illness had been in remission, but early in the new year it took a turn for the worse. The muscles in his legs and arms tightened making movement difficult to control. A sprightly eighty-year old in November, by January he had become a semi-invalid. Still, he continued with his daily walk and one morning set out across the cobbles that now hurt his feet and threatened to unbalance him. The slight rise to the city centre left him panting. As he paused to catch his breath he noticed a group of men outside the

Jobcentre and Benefits Office, some holding cans of beer. They were being addressed by a tall, grey-haired figure. It was Miles. As Tom passed them, the group turned to watch his slow progress.

A few days later Tom was leaving his house for his daily walk when Miles came up to him.

'I'd be honoured if in return for the kindness you've shown me you would join me for a coffee,' he said.

Despite his doubts, Tom felt it would be churlish to refuse, and they walked across the road, down the flight of stairs, the older man resting on the younger's arm. The room had been tidied, the glass removed from the table, where a cafetière of coffee had been placed, with cups and some homemade cakes.

'That's quite a following you had at the Benefits Office,' said Tom, taking a sip of coffee and a bite of cake.

'Well, you know, once a teacher always a teacher....' Tom looked at Miles enquiringly, but he did not elaborate, and instead began to sketch the past history of their street, the Victorian leather workshops in the terraced cottages, the eighteenth century pub on the corner, the old children's hospital. Unaccountably, as he listened, Tom felt the gloom of these last weeks of illness lifting. And looking at Miles it was easy to see him, now, as a teacher, even as a professor. He spoke with confidence and gravitas. The long grey hair fell in waves to the shoulder and together with the recently grown beard gave to the face a definite note of distinction.

As Tom helped himself to more coffee and cakes, he felt a warmth suffuse his body, relaxing the tightened muscles of his arms and legs. He looked out of the window and was surprised to find the gable ends of his house lit with a new clarity. The yellow ochre of the rendered walls, the curving pantiles on the roof, even the water marks on the columns of his neighbour's porch, all seemed new and touched with a radiance he had never noticed. But there was something wrong, a crease in one of the red velvet curtains in his bedroom window.

'There was this woman, Miles,' he began, 'who used to look at the top windows in Buckingham Palace, and every time a curtain moved she thought that George V was sending her a sign.' At that moment the two men saw Sue coming to the window. She too must have noticed the disarray of the curtains. With a twitch she restored them to perfect symmetry. 'There you are Miles, a message from your secret admirer.' They burst into laughter. When finally he got up to leave, Tom found his muscles had relaxed and he could move with a freedom he hadn't felt for months.

In the weeks that followed, the offer of coffee and cakes was often renewed by Miles, and Tom's condition went into remission once more. From his upstairs bedroom he would see on certain days that the curtains had been drawn and a cafetière and plates set out on the little table in Miles' sitting room. Unfailingly an invitation would arrive. He got in the habit of looking out of his window every day hoping for this sign of the pleasure and release to come. Coffee mornings with Miles were devoted to discussions of politics and history, at least until talk lapsed into silent states of mindfulness.

It was Tom who found Miles' body. On an early morning errand to Kate and Martin's he entered the tunnel to see a long shape laid out on the cobbles half way along. As he got closer, he recognized the khaki coat and brown trousers. The long grey hair was now matted in blood. Once more Tom had to call for an ambulance before checking for signs of life. This time it was hopeless. The investigation that followed concluded that the death was drugs related. Between six in the morning and ten at night the tunnel was a cheerful people's palace of art, but after midnight it became a sinister venue where hooded men in muttering groups struck deals. Occasionally there would be outbreaks of violence. The detective assigned to the case said that Miles' supplier had probably wanted to teach him a lesson for not paying his debts and the beating had triggered a stroke.

In the weeks that followed Tom was plagued by an awful possibility. Those cakes that made his visits to Miles so enjoyable. Had Miles been unable to meet the payments for whatever it was that filled them? Had he paid with his life trying to keep their coffee mornings supplied? The funeral was held in the city cemetery a mile or so from the underpass. On a raw March morning Tom and a few of Miles' friends from the Benefits Office watched his body being put into the grave. At the little service in the cemetery chapel a locum curate had given a brief address. He talked of the brilliant student Miles had been, of his long years as a teacher, the steady upward progress of his career, his current chairmanship of the local history society and of many professional associations in the city, of 'a life crowned with many achievements'. Tom marvelled at the sheer inventiveness of the eulogy, and at the reception after he approached the speaker.

'Of course, I didn't know the man from Adam,' said the curate holding up a sheet of paper, 'but among his things they found this very helpful summary which he'd written, with instructions that it should be read out at his funeral.'

Months later, on a warm summer's day, Tom decided to take a walk in the cemetery where Miles was buried. He made his way to the site of the grave, but nowhere could he see the modest memorial he was expecting, only a neo-classical monument he assumed was from the nineteenth century. A closer look showed the mottled marble to be shiny and new. On it the words 'Sacred to the memory of Miles Cunningham, gentleman of this City', in gleaming gold, were followed by a shortened version of the funeral eulogy. In the shape of a portico, with columns holding up an architrave and cornice, the memorial would clearly last for decades, indeed centuries.

Soft Power

At the door of the plane Nathan was met by a gust of hot, fumy, dust-filled air. Half-closing his eyes to the glare of the sun, he descended the stairway, pausing to take in his first view of Africa, the reddish hills in the distance, the palms skirting the airport. At the foot of the stairs he waited for his wife Elaine, with their daughter Emily in her arms, and together they crossed the asphalt to the shade and cool of the airport arrivals hall. There, amid the bright figure-hugging prints of the women and the robes of the men, they saw a frail, slim, white figure, at a guess in his fifties. He was dressed in a cream short-sleeved shirt and rust-coloured trousers, the creases immaculately pressed, his blond hair slicked down into a neat side parting. A pale wraith amidst the vibrant colours of the hall. Next to him was a short black man with powerful arms and shoulders, dressed in white shorts and singlet. One arm circled a bouquet of flowers, the other held a sign with their names. As they approached, the white man came forward and introduced himself.

'Mr. and Mrs. Trent? I am Professor Howard. Welcome to Africa! Give the flowers to the lady, Malone.'

'Yes Massa, I give them to madam quick quick.'

Taken aback, Elaine received the bunch of red hibiscus, soft blue bougainvillea and cream frangipani.

They waited while Professor Howard and Malone went to see to their luggage.

'Massa?' she whispered to Nathan. 'Shades of Uncle Tom's Cabin! Let's get the next plane back to England.' But they didn't.

Nathan had arrived with his wife and three-year old daughter to take up a lecturing post in English at the University of Sigania. It was September 1970, a year after that decade of change in Britain which had ended with student marches and sit-ins. Nathan decided he needed a break from PhD studies and student politics at UCL, and when the chance arose of a two-year post in a West African country whose struggle for independence had always inspired him, he jumped at it.

On the drive from the airport Professor Howard took them through the centre of the city, skirting the main market where they looked with wonder at stalls of brightly coloured cloth, enamel kitchen ware, slabs of meat, yam, cassava, avocado, pineapples. Through the open window they smelled the rich odour of refuse rotting in huge roadside storm drains and heard snatches of high life music, cries of hawkers. Gradually this riot of the senses receded and after a short journey they entered the gates of the university campus.

'Civilisation, at last,' said Professor Howard. Halls of residence, imposing buildings with whitewashed walls and red-tiled roofs, rose on a gentle incline, steepening into a small hill at the top of which a campanile overlooked the peaceful scene. Between the halls were grassy spaces with ornamental ponds and staff bungalows and at one of them the Trents were deposited. It was to be their temporary home while permanent accommodation was prepared. A university driver would collect them for dinner in three hours.

It was dark by the time they arrived at Professor Howard's bungalow. Their host, cigarette in hand, led them into a softly lit room, where through the open French windows the chirring of cicadas and the croaking of frogs entered from a small garden. The three-year-old, already asleep, was taken to an adjoining room.

'Sundowners!' said Howard, pouring two large whisky and sodas, and, afraid to offend their host, Nathan and Elaine accepted them. Hardly had they sat down when the telephone rang.

'Absolutely impossible,' said Howard to the caller. 'Out of the question. Totally exhausted after their long flight you see. Goodbye.' He put down the telephone: 'Huh,' he said with a sneer, 'that was the Serpent.'

Dr. Sarpong, or the Serpent as Howard called him, was his African deputy in the English department and naturally anxious to meet his new colleague, but Howard had resisted.

'Can't wait to put his oar in. Thinks he should have been head of department and been scheming ever since I got here. They're not ready for it yet. You have to be born into a culture to be able to teach it properly.'

Nathan was about to raise an objection when Malone entered with dinner, and over dishes of roast pork and yam croquettes, Nathan and Elaine were treated to Howard's views on how literature should be taught. As whisky followed whisky, his mouth became fixed in a sneer, the eyes narrowed into slits, the voice began to slur, the hand with the cigarette to shake, and when Nathan offered an opinion, Howard bristled:

'We want them to learn how to love and quote Wordsworth, not to dissect him.'

'You mean you want your students to become

cultivated English gentlemen,' said Nathan, barely able to keep the scorn out of his voice.

'Precisely,' said Howard.

The situation was becoming ugly, when, from the open French window, a boy of about nine entered. The faded singlet and shorts could not detract from the child's beauty. A broad forehead emphasised the large brown eyes and the high cheek bones over perfectly sculpted lips.

'Ah, there you are Awudu,' said Howard, and, getting up shakily, ushered him into an adjoining room. Nathan and Elaine looked at each other. After some minutes of muffled conversation, Howard and Awudu emerged from the room and the boy, a wad of banknotes in his hand, disappeared through the French windows into the night. No explanation was offered by Howard and when a whimper from the bedroom announced that Emily had awoken, the Trents made their apologies and left.

The Serpent turned out to be a tall African lecturer of forty with a doctorate from Cambridge, who lived on the campus with his wife and three-year old son. Having children of the same age at the university nursery school, the Trents got to know Kofi, his wife Efua and their son Yao, and, once settled in their own bungalow at the edge of campus, they would exchange social visits. One evening, as Efua was teaching Elaine how to cook palm nut soup and *fufu*, Kofi and Nathan were seated around the Trents' ornamental pond, watching the children at play.

'Of course economic development is important,' Kofi was saying, 'but with it comes the duty to manage all that material progress fairly, honestly and morally and that's where literature comes in, that's why we need Dickens,

Lawrence, yes and our own Achebe, Armah, … Heh Yao and Emily! Keep away from the water. You don't want to be ponded do you?'

'Ponded?' asked Nathan.

'One of our traditions. If our students feel that someone, however important or powerful, has committed an outrage, they gather together and take the offender to one of our ornamental ponds and throw him in. It happened last year to a big shot Nigerian executive appointed to run the refectory. He refused to listen to the students' complaints about the food, and… well, he was ponded. They say he emerged from the muddy water with his head garlanded in lilies and no doubt having swallowed lots of tadpoles and newts.'

After Christmas the arrival of the dry season heralded the annual event that most raised the profile of the English Department, the series of classic films organised by the British Council. That year it was to be the National Theatre production of *Othello* with Olivier in the lead.

The students gather in the lecture hall, many of them dressed in formal traditional clothes for the occasion, wearing the richly coloured Kente cloth like a Roman toga with one end over a shoulder. After a short introduction by Professor Howard, the film begins. As Othello speaks of being taken by the insolent foe and sold to slavery, a murmur of sympathy runs through the mainly African students and lecturers. Their eyes are fixed on the noble moor, on the strong features of the blackened face, the confident bearing, the dark robe over a white undershirt weighed down by the heavy chain of office. The figure exudes presence. Before him the assembly of Venetian nobles pale into insignificance. A cheer rings out as they watch Othello announce the destruction of the Turkish fleet and lead Desdemona to their nuptial bed. An attaché at the British High Commission leans over to Nathan and whispers: 'That's what you call "soft power". Who needs China's billion dollar investments when we have our luvvies? Good old Will.'

As the film progresses, there is a shift of feeling in the audience. They follow Iago's easy manipulation of Othello with increasing concern, the black man made the plaything of the scheming Venetian, and note how Othello's dignified bearing has given way to ugly grimaces and a feral swaying of the hips. Murmurings of disapproval. Then the moment when, racked by jealous suspicions, Othello loses coherence and falls into a fit. Olivier has developed a line of stage direction into a bravura performance of epilepsy, with the rolling of red-rimmed eyes, pupils disappearing into his forehead, thrashing of limbs, garbling of words, and finally a body trapped in paralysis, with the white man standing over it. There is uproar. Cries of 'Insult! Insult!' The banging of desk lids reaches a crescendo and the film is brought to an end as a number of students and faculty leave shouting abuse. Nathan and Elaine have watched the film before and marvelled at Olivier, but now, in that audience, they see it differently.

Professor Howard takes to the podium, lips pressed tightly, white with anger, hands visibly shaking, and glowers at the remaining lecturers and students. The midday whisky, perfect prop for his genial introduction, is now fuelling a venomous malice.

'Today Sigania has disgraced herself,' he begins. 'Your fellow students and (sneering) lecturers have shown themselves unworthy of the highest forms of art, unable to appreciate a feat of acting by a genius at the height of his powers. What better compliment to Africa than to see Laurence Olivier enter into the mind of an African, indeed into his very body.' There is uproar. The remaining audience members, some in formal robes, some in trousers and short-sleeved shirts approach the podium menacingly. Nathan sees the danger and helped by the British diplomat quickly rushes to the podium, guiding Professor Howard, by now quite unsteady on his feet, to an exit behind the stage and podium.

Next day, reaction throughout the university was instant and extreme. On his way to the English meeting scheduled for that morning, Nathan noticed a banner outside the Institute of African Studies: 'Department of English – last bastion of racist cultural imperialism'. Outside a hall of residence, a large group of students was being addressed by a student leader.

'The liberation of Africa will be incomplete until we have expelled the colonialist and all his African stooges from our beloved country.' He ended with a cutting thrust of his arm, and a shout of approval went through the crowd.

At the Department office, Nathan found expatriate and African lecturers in animated discussion of the last night's events impatiently waiting for the meeting to begin. At last Professor Howard entered, defiant, fortified, holding a copy of Matthew Arnold's *Culture and Anarchy* high in the air. 'The Barbarians are at our door,' he began, but at that moment nature got the better of culture, and, obeying her call, knees clenched, he backed to the door and, with a final wave of Matthew Arnold, exited the room. The whole room, African and expatriate lecturers, student reps, department secretary, burst into laughter.

After the meeting Kofi approached Nathan in some distress. A petition signed by some hundred faculty and students had been presented to the university senate demanding the abolition of the English Department as a 'vehicle of Neo-Colonialism'. The petition was likely to be supported and the Department of English abolished.

'We have to head off the petition,' said Kofi. 'We have to disassociate ourselves from the Prof. A group of us have put together an alternative petition condemning his racist views as a misrepresentation of the English department and demanding his replacement by an African Head of Department. If you were to join us and sign the petition, Nathan, it would show we're not motivated by narrow anti-white sentiments.' A decision was needed urgently as the petition was going to be presented the next day.

That evening wife and husband discussed the situation.

'From what you say,' began Elaine, 'Howard's lost all respect among the lecturers and students and it's time for the better man to take over. Kofi has such exciting ideas. I've heard him talk about widening the syllabus – books from Africa, India, the Caribbean as well as Britain. He'd be an inspiring leader. Can't you see?'

'I know, I know,' said Nathan wearily, 'but it would seem such an act of treachery, signing the petition. I can imagine what Howard would say, "Gone over to Sarpong, beguiled by the sly Serpent". And he has been kind to us. Flowers for you when we arrived and more flowers after your bout of malaria.'

'Gestures, gestures, romantic nonsense. What about that pretty young boy we saw on our first night at Howard's, Awudu was it? What's going on there?' The Trents had never referred to that scene before, its implications too awful to contemplate. 'You've got to think about what's best for your students.'

Back at UCL Nathan had found it so simple to lead a demonstration or organise a protest. Why did he feel so conflicted now? Finally he decided to go over to Kofi's bungalow and sign the petition. On his return he saw a figure waiting for him outside the garden. It was Emmanuel, a student he had got to know when starting up a creative writing group.

'I am sorry to disturb you so late,' he began, 'but I have just heard they are planning to pond Professor Howard tomorrow morning. I do not feel this is right and I think you should warn the Prof.'

'I see,' said Nathan. 'Will you come in and give me some more details? Have a coffee or a beer?'

'Thank you, no. Just now it is not good for me to be seen at the house of a European lecturer. I will leave now.'

It was obvious what Nathan had to do. It was only ten o'clock, plenty of time to walk over to Howard's bungalow and warn him. Elaine looked at him questioningly.

'Let me think about it,' he said, pouring himself a Club beer.

'Well, I'm going to bed.'

If word got out that he had tipped off the Prof, Nathan would be seen to have sided with the Englishman against the Africans. Was it right to prevent the students expressing their justified resentment? He poured himself another beer and then another. They would probably just chant some slogans outside Howard's bungalow and leave. With every beer he drank he felt more confident that everything would turn out well the next day. Finally he fell asleep on the sofa.

He awoke next morning with a vague sense of unease. Then he remembered. It was the day of the ponding of Professor Howard. Some time that morning an angry crowd of students would surround his bungalow and demand to see him. When the Prof failed to appear they would break in. The loyal Malone, for all his muscularity, would offer little protection. They would carry the struggling Englishman to the large pond outside the university library and throw his frail body into the water. What ignominy, thought Nathan, as he imagined Howard, muddy faced, hair garlanded with water lilies, struggling to get out. To distract himself from such painful images Nathan went into the bedroom to switch on Radio Sigania. The morning talk show, with its mixture of highlife numbers, snippets of local news, jokes and interviews always raised his spirits, but what he heard was music, an unbroken sequence of stirring marches. Nathan rushed back into the dining room and looked enquiringly at their maid Esther who was setting out breakfast (for the Trents for all their socialist convictions had employed a maid).

'Is a coup,' she said. 'Soldiers fed up with all the shortages in the shops. They always play that kind of music when there is a coup.'

Nathan dressed quickly and made for the English department. At the main gate of the university a tank had been positioned. Surrounding it were soldiers carrying sub-machine guns. From the direction of the library further up the hill, he could hear the noise of an angry crowd and rushing there found a group of students gathered in front of the library preventing entry to the soldiers. For the soldiers, the library with its whitewashed walls and tiered red-tiled roofs summed up the privileged world of the university on its hill-top haven. They were determined to enter and take possession of it. Two of them advanced and grabbed a student, pushed him to the ground and began to beat him with baton and rifle butt.

'Should I intervene?' wondered Nathan, but he did not.

The clamour of the crowd intensified. Suddenly there was a lull. The crowd parted to let in a slight white figure, a thin arm held high in admonition. It was Professor Howard, closely followed by Malone. 'Stop that! Stop that at once!' shouted Howard, his voice turned falsetto by the emotion of the occasion. The two soldiers paused in disbelief, but only for a moment before the larger one stepped forward and with a heave of his shoulder sent Howard sprawling. He then began to beat the Englishman. There was a cry of dismay from the students. A taboo had been broken, a guest in their land assaulted. The line between a civil society and a regime of violence had been crossed. Resistance was over and the soldiers swarmed into the library. Malone rushed to help Howard and was immediately set upon by more soldiers wielding batons and rifle butts.

The soldiers' triumph was short-lived. A student had taken a photo of the incident, and, sold to the Daily Graphic, it made the front page next day, syndicated to Reuters. A powerful African soldier with baton raised above the frail body of a white man. It was one of those images that change public opinion nationally and internationally. The coup leaders knew that while world opinion might tolerate some brutality to their own African students, the spectacle of violence to Europeans would cause alarm and endanger development aid. An order went out that violence, to expatriates and to students, was to be avoided at all costs and that the library be returned to university control.

The next morning Nathan made his way to Howard's bungalow to find it surrounded by a hundred or so students singing a traditional song of victory. When the Prof appeared outside, his pale face blazoned with purple bruises, a group of them, taking great care to avoid the painful ribs, hoisted him onto their shoulders. They carried him to the library, the scene of his courageous stand, and set him down by the huge ornamental pond that faced the entrance. Here he made a short speech, saying how proud he was to have joined his students in their resistance to the forces of barbarism.

'From this day to the ending of the world we shall be remembered,' he concluded, 'we few, we happy few, we band of brothers... and sisters.' Cheers.

Nathan had felt himself an ignominious onlooker on the fringes of Howard's triumph. Soon his signature on the petition and the betrayal of his colleague would be known throughout the university. He decided to pay his head of department a visit that afternoon. Howard was seated in his usual chair, cigarette in hand, a whisky by his side, being ministered to by Malone; the white bandage on Malone's head a perfect accessory to the shorts and singlet. After enquiring about Howard's health, Nathan informed Howard that he had decided to resign, that he and Elaine would be returning to England early, at the end of the term.

'Really, is that so?' said Howard and thought for a moment. 'Well, perhaps you're right. Quite frankly, Nathan, I'm not sure you're cut out for this job. It's a big responsibility representing your country and standing up for her values.'

At that moment, two figures walked into the room from the garden balcony. One of them was the young boy Awudu, the other a much older man, leaning on a stick.

'Ah Ohene, do come in,' said Howard to the older man. 'Good to see you recovered from the bout of hepatitis. That was nasty.' Then, turning to Nathan, 'This is Ohene, Malone's illustrious predecessor.'

The old man moved forward. 'I come to thank you, sir. The money you sent by my grandson help me buy medicine. It cure me. Thank you, Thank you.'

Nathan took his leave, glad to have discovered that his suspicions about Howard and the young boy had proved false. Back in the department he found Kofi at his typewriter.

'I've just got back from an emergency session of the Senate, Nathan,' he said. 'They've passed a formal vote of thanks to Professor Howard for his courageous stand in defence of the students. The petition to close the English department has been rejected, and so of course has the one to replace Howard. My position is impossible, and I'm typing my letter of resignation. I had hoped to serve my country to the end of my life, teaching literature to its young people, but the good lord has thought otherwise.'

'Surely,' protested Nathan, 'things will settle down soon and you and Howard will be able to go on as before?'

'Never. I tried to remove him when he was vulnerable. They will all see that as an attempted coup, and you know what happens to the leaders of a failed coup.'

Later in his life Nathan often found his thoughts returning to the day of Professor Howard's triumph and Kofi Sarpong's resignation. Then in 2020, many years after his own retirement from teaching, he made an online search and found this entry: 'It is with great sadness that the Sarpong family announce the death of Professor Kofi Sarpong. In his long career he had been an inspiration to many students in universities throughout Africa. It was his deepest desire to return to teach in his home land of Sigania and it is therefore right that his body should be brought back and laid to rest not far from the university where he began his career....' Searches for

Professor Howard were less productive. A handful of brief references to him in universities in Singapore, South Korea, Botswana, showed him continuing to represent his country and her values for many years.

The Body in the Garden

'There's a body out there! In our garden!'

When my wife made her announcement, standing at our front window that warm summer evening, I was surprised but not incredulous. After all, in a terrace bookended by a pub and a bistro, our garden was often a receptacle for abandoned things. Beer mugs, wine glasses, half-eaten burgers, once a child's buggy with a bent wheel. Still, a body. That was something else. Joining her at the window, I could see it plainly. A long pale shape in the shade of the magnolia tree that takes up most of our front garden. We rushed out. The body of a young woman was laid out on the round pebbles between tree and front wall: tee shirt, shorts, trainers; dark hair framing a sweet, almost childish face, grubby now; hands grasping a mobile. There were red marks on her shins where she must have grazed herself clambering over a low wall of sharp-edged flints onto the bed of pebbles. Eyes closed, her body, in the foetal position, was perfectly still.

I had a fleeting sense of pride that, of all the front gardens, she had chosen ours for her resting place, that she had entrusted herself to us, but quickly the enormity of the scene dawned on me. Was she alive or dead? I raised my hand to shake her, then paused, restrained by some inner taboo. And what if she was dead? – police cars, garden taped off, neighbours' suspicions... but then I shook, she stirred, and it became another scene. I shook again and the young woman mumbled something about 'home', wanting to get there. There was the hint of a foreign accent. Home. But where? With infinite care I helped her from under the magnolia branches, over the flint wall, out of the gate and onto the pavement. A few uncertain steps took her to a little convenience store run by a family of Kurds. She entered. Safe, I hoped, in her own community. To make sure, we followed, only to find her laid out, unconscious, by the shelves along the far wall, next to dishwasher tablets and kitchen rolls. The shopkeeper stood over her, concerned, perplexed. Clearly he did not know her. We all looked at each other.

'Have to be the police, I suppose,' said my wife. The horror on the shopkeeper's face mirrored my own. I was thinking forcible repatriation, detention centres. At that moment the young woman's mobile rang. She stirred.

'Home, I want go back,' she said, but did not answer her phone. So I did.

'What the hell are you playing at, Lina? Where are you for god's sake? I've been desperately worried.' The male voice on the phone was worried but also angry. I explained who and where I was and the voice became calmer.

'She's very vulnerable, you see. Manages most of the time, but then something like this kicks off. Completely off her face for hours, days.'

'Drugs?' I offered.

'Oh no, no, no....no! Alcohol, always alcohol. Big problem in Lithuania... where she comes from.' Strange that I had missed the smell of alcohol when I helped Lina to her feet. 'Look,' he went on, 'the best thing you can do is to take her to her place. It's thirty-seven Albion Road.

Landlady will take care of her. Wonderful lady. She's a…a mental health nurse. Could you manage that?'

I jumped at his suggestion. 'Yes, of course.'

He seemed unconvinced. 'You will get her there won't you? You need to get her there as soon as possible.'

'Don't worry. Will do, straightaway,' I said, giving him our address so he could check up about Lina later that evening.

Grateful that someone had taken responsibility, I explained the plan to my wife.

'But who is this man?' she said. 'We need to check, make sure he's kosher.'

'Oh, come *on*, don't be such a cynic,' I countered. 'He sounded bright, educated. Let's go.'

We found Albion Road on Google Maps, not somewhere near us as we had assumed, but on the outskirts of the city several miles away. No matter. It was a crisis and we were on a mission. An adrenalin rush had wiped away the torpor of the hot summer evening.

With Lina safely strapped in on the back seat we drove to the steep hill that overlooks the city. Half way up was Albion Road, a long narrow street of terraced houses with cars parked close together. Unable to find a space I drove on to where houses gave way to the city prison and parked opposite. We needed to check that the landlady was in, so I got out of the car and made my way past groups of men with cans of beer, relaxing in the prison car park. Perhaps privileged inmates and their friends. Amidst the neatly kept front gardens on Albion Road number thirty-seven's stood out. A tall laurel hedge almost hid the faded purple front door and behind the hedge I could make out a jumble of objects, a ladder, a folding bed. I knocked once, twice. The door was opened by a large woman, perhaps in her fifties. She was wearing a nightdress and dressing gown in some silky material and held a cigarette.

'Done it again has she?' she said after I explained the situation. 'Okay, let's go.'

She stamped out the cigarette with her slipper and we walked in silence back to the car. Refusing offers of help, she opened the door, lifted Lina from the car and, her shoulder under one of the young woman's arms, began to walk her back to the house while I hovered ineffectually. An arm draped around her landlady's neck, Lina hung, limp and waiflike, against the bulk of the older woman, her stuttering steps trying to keep pace with the other's long strides. A hush fell upon the beer drinkers as we passed until some comment prompted a burst of jeering laughter. On reaching her house the landlady took out the key with her free hand to open the door and Lina turned to look at me. For a moment our eyes met. Back at the car I noticed for the first time the imposing façade of the prison illuminated by the evening sun, its two tall clock towers seeming to keep guard. Despite the warmth of the evening, a shiver ran through me.

On our return we found a young man waiting outside our front gate. In his late twenties, he was stylishly dressed in blouson, close-fitting jeans and trainers and carried a canvas hold-all.

'Hi, I'm Peter, Peter Story,' he began. 'Are you the guys who helped Lina? I just wanted to say you've been absolutely amazing.' It was the voice of the man on the phone. 'I've been so worried about Lina. Known her for years. We were together once, but... well... I still see her regularly though. I'm a student at the university, European politics, got a part-time job at the Co-op down the road close to my flat.'

And then the details poured forth in one fluent, articulate stream: meeting Lina while researching in Kaunas, Lithuania; her alcohol addiction, the suicide attempts and self-harming; his visits to the asylum where she'd been confined; seeing her handcuffed to her bed; the oppressive mental health system in Eastern Europe.

When I interrupted to ask if the Social Services here were helping her he seemed annoyed. 'No, she's got a job at the burger bar in the city's shopping centre. She can handle things most of the time and doesn't need people to interfere.' He paused and then, 'Look I found this bag by your front wall; it's hers. She must have left it there. You couldn't ... possibly ... take it to her, could you?'

I was ready to agree but he noticed my wife's reaction. 'That's okay, you've done enough. I'll get it to her somehow.' With that he turned and we watched him make his way up our road towards where he said his flat was.

'Well, that's some impressive young man,' I said to my wife when he was out of earshot. 'Lina's so lucky to have him looking out for her.'

'What?!' she said. 'You didn't buy it all did you? You didn't find him a bit much, a bit domineering?'

'Well,' I said, 'intense perhaps.'

'Manic,' she replied.

'Look,' I pointed out, 'he obviously cares a lot for Lina.'

'He certainly cares a lot about what happens to her and who deals with her. And drunk?! She wasn't drunk. Not a whiff of alcohol. Drugs more like. He's probably her supplier and terrified the police will get involved. A vulnerable woman with a drug dependency... he could get her to do anything. And why did he come here with the bag? He wanted to check up on us. We didn't see any bag outside the gate, did we? He had it in his digs and was desperate to get rid of it in case it connected him to her.'

'Pure speculation,' I said. 'God, you've got a vivid imagination.'

'And what about the 'landlady' – in her silk peignoir at 6 p.m?'

'Oh come off it. Are you saying she was dressed like that to welcome her clients? On Albion Road? She's a psychiatric nurse not the Madam of a bordello. She probably does shift work at the mental hospital and has to sleep during the day.'

'Well then, that group of men laughing suggestively when she passed with Lina? They know exactly what goes on at number thirty-seven.'

'Probably not laughing at her at all, but at the idiot tagging along behind her like a spare part. The way she hefted Lina from car to house, a good forty yards. Heroic I'd call it.'

'You didn't find it ... a bit proprietorial?'

'Look,' I said finally, trying to make light of the evening. 'There's a perfectly innocent explanation for everything that happened tonight and I prefer that to your sinister fantasies. A young woman has a bit too much to drink and gets in a pickle, or, rather, gets pickled. We do our civic duty and help out. That's it. Job done.'

But it wasn't. In the days that followed I couldn't stop thinking about what had happened. That last look that Lina gave me took on a heavier and heavier significance. What did it mean? I thought I had been on a heroic mission to Albion Road but what if I had instead delivered her into the hands of her exploiters? I had to find out and began to investigate. At the University's Department of Politics they had no record of a student named Peter Story. I did my shopping at the Co-op where Peter said he worked, but no sign of him. Burgers are not my preferred choice of dish, but I spent evenings eating them at the bar where Lina was supposed to serve. She never showed up. I decided to confront Lina's landlady and made my way to Albion Road once more. The folding bed and ladder had been removed from the front garden of number thirty-seven and there was a sign announcing the date of an auction on October the fifth. I looked in at the window and saw that the front room had been cleared of furniture. At this point, if I were in a novel or film, there would be a lead leading to another lead and then another until finally the object of the quest would be found and the truth revealed. In my case the leads had petered out. Of course there could be an innocent explanation for everything, but the alternative was painful to contemplate. As I did, often; the sweet childish face; the last look she gave me; and her words, the only time Lina had spoken, 'Home, I want go back.'

N10 goes 6 Degrees North

She should have bought the Roquefort and Époisses herself. Details mattered and the dinner party had to be perfect – simple cottage pie, Eton mess, Emma Bridgwater dishware, with a hint of distinction from the expensive French cheese and a vintage Sauternes: understated North London chic she had gradually mastered since arriving from her Midland town in 1997. Yes, the dinner party had to be perfect. Everything, her future, Jerry's, their daughter's, depended on the chief guest, her father-in-law Gordon. Would he agree to the plan? Brenda imagined him: the familiar sports jacket, open-necked shirt, hair a mass of untidy curls; the accent that always reminded her of the past she wanted to escape. He would be feeling tired after the recent flight from West Africa. She must do everything to make him feel at home, cosseted. Should she have sent that note asking him to pick up the cheese from Borough market on his way to the dinner party tonight? The thought niggled all day.

It was to be a busy morning. At ten thirty the financial adviser. The crash that followed the pandemic had meant some adjustments if her and Jerry's life plan was to be kept on track. Then at twelve, it was open day at the expensive private school near the Embankment to which she was determined to send Emma next year. On the way back, fresh strawberries from Covent Garden market, and perhaps some table titivation, fragrant candles. Men of a certain age could be so susceptible.

At eight thirty, she left her Muswell Hill home in Goldborne Gardens, stopping for a moment at Alexandra Palace, before the short walk to the bus that would take her into central London. She stood in front of the fire-ravaged arches of the people's palace, close to the vast rose window in its neo-classical frame, seeing the whole of the city, impossibly foreshortened. The view never failed to lift her spirits, made her feel eager to plunge into the fight again. Haringey, Islington, Finsbury Park, Caledonian Road, Holborn, the Gherkin and Shard; and to the left, just visible, a cluster of skyscrapers on Canary Wharf, their tops gilded by the bright sun, where her husband worked in the investment arm of an international bank. At this memory her stomach wrenched. How much longer before security would appear at Jerry's desk and escort him from the building? Brushing aside these thoughts she imagined the river as it snaked its way to the sea, past Rotherhithe, the Isle of Dogs, Greenwich, and Gravesend. What great projects had not sailed from that great river into the rest of the world, companies, colonies, empires...?

As the bus passed through Crouch End the clock tower showed nine. She was comfortably seated on the lower deck of the bus from where she could observe the arriving passengers. It was two years since the pandemic, and the streets had long resumed the variety that never failed to excite her: an Ashanti mother and father robed in the blue, red and gold colours of Kente; two fine-featured Somali boys, profiles of carved ebony, silent; a group of Asian youths and their friend in the black and white keffiyeh she always found vaguely threatening, arguing loudly. Outside, the shop fronts rushed past – Halal butchers,

Polski Skleps, import-export businesses to Syria and the Lebanon, foreign exchange shops offering good rates for the Naira and Cedi, endless hair salons. She sometimes wondered if she was right to protect her two children quite so fiercely from this vivid human spectacle. Their junior school had certainly been multinational but the fees had guaranteed an intake sharing the taste and style of a new global élite. Children of Swedish IT executives, American hedge fund managers, Japanese bankers, Arab entrepreneurs, dressed by Little Liberty and Jessie and James, ferried from school to home in Freelanders and Shoguns, insulated from the street by tinted glass and heavy doors. She imagined the common life pattern of health clubs, West End first nights, Covent Garden, Ascot, Wimbledon, the Lord's Test.

Ten o'clock and the bus passed Pentonville prison, its entrance like a mediaeval barbican, the barred cell windows just visible over high whitewashed walls. Of course, the city had been 'one of the dark places of the earth' she remembered and felt grateful once more for the cordon sanitaire that she and Jerry had constructed against a threatening world.

It was at ten that her husband Jerry had a meeting with his bank's Development Unit. The pandemic had left the derivatives market pretty moribund, and if he was to justify his bonus this year he needed to find a sector where the yields were more attractive. No bonus, no school fees, it was as simple as that. And furthermore, no nanny, no personal trainer, nor any of the other life aids taken for granted in the set in which they moved. Probably no sex too. Certainly not the more adventurous moves that Brenda and he had been practising under the guidance of their newspaper's sexual advice column, the Goldborne variations he had quipped with his PA. Inspiration had come over a drink at his father's local. His father Gordon, part merchant venturer, part wheeler-dealer, part philanthropist, told a rousing tale of business opportunities in Africa: how Chinese and South African firms were scooping up the pickings as the continent began to realise its huge potential. His father's own company, Trans Tropics Partnership, ran a successful scheme in the Brong Ahafo region of Ghana, providing crop management, milling, processing and transport services to indigenous palm oil farmers. Although a commercial company, it had a wider social remit and his father described enthusiastically how some of the profits were being spent on new schools, electricity, water supplies, clinics. Jerry had bridled at the idea of ethical investing, all that workers' co-operative stuff, exasperated as always by the naïve idealism his father never seemed to have outgrown, but he listened with feigned interest while the outline of a new investment scheme began to form in his mind. A fortnight later, after meetings with an old business school friend, now CEO of Caerleon Capital, and some due diligence with the finances of Trans Tropics, Jerry stood at the door of his bank's Development Unit, armed with a glossy business plan and rehearsed the PowerPoint presentation which was to launch his foray into Africa. His mobile buzzed the 10.00 reminder call.

At that moment Jerry's father Gordon was at the Stepney post office with a bulky parcel.

'It's got to go with the ten o'clock post today,' he said with some irritation to the cashier as she weighed it. A persistent temperature since arriving from Accra had made him unusually tetchy. The parcel contained a new mini-fridge he had promised to send Kwabena, the elderly farmer he had grown fond of in the Brong Ahafo scheme. Gordon remembered his first meeting with the village council, on a circle of stools under a tree on the swept dried mud of the village centre surrounded by dusty-white walls of compounds. He had explained how Trans Tropics would invest in and restore palm oil production in the village from its present state of neglect. TT would repair the purpose built mill and provide transport, cultivation and harvesting services for those who joined the co-operative. Incomes would be doubled and profits used to improve local services.

'Where there be much profit, there be many mouths to eat it,' said one of the villagers, cynical and suspicious, summing up the general mood, but Kwabena had brought them round and helped to organize the villagers into an effective co-operative. On his recent visit, Gordon found the farms transformed, the trees correctly pruned, their fronds like inverted fan tails, forming neat rows, the black nuggets of the fruit glistening inside. Already, as income increased, farming was shifting from survival and subsistence to relative prosperity, improved amenities, a few luxuries, and the space for a more relaxed communal life closer to that of their ancestors.

On the plane back to London Gordon, still full of the project's success, bombarded a young mother who had joined the flight earlier at Kinshasa with details of the scheme, his enthusiasm eventually overcoming her natural modesty and reticence. In her buba with matching skirt and dress, Efua was a picture of elegance. Plaits were carefully arranged to fall gracefully from her head onto her bosom, across which an open-work stole of some leather material, decorated with cowries, set off the discreet gold necklace. The child at her side had become fretful, his eyes inflamed, joints aching, during the long flight over the Sahara, and Gordon, with his old coaster's claim to medical knowhow, confidently diagnosed a slight touch of malaria. His genuine concern for Obi, the little boy, overcame any lingering social barriers and when he produced some Artemesin tablets for what seemed like mild fever and tiredness, the young mother was overwhelmed with gratitude, sought contact details to return his kindness and expenses.

'Achieving academic excellence is a goal for every girl here, but so too is developing individual talents and interests.' Brenda nodded with approval as she caught the school principal's opening words while trying to find a seat in the assembly hall's bright modern décor, surrounded by media suites like chapels in a mediaeval cathedral. But as the talk continued, 'We encourage girls to broaden their horizons. Our programme of Community Service, our thriving participation in the Duke of Edinburgh Award Scheme and our partnerships with London state schools and colleges all help the girls to develop personal responsibility and respect for others...,' Brenda began to feel some anxiety. The ex-conservatoire cello teacher, home lessons with Oxbridge science and maths graduates, holiday schools for gifted children – did all that commitment of money, time and energy really leave room for worthy projects that might distract Emma from her drive to the top? She quickly dispelled these doubts to concentrate on the looming present: after the meeting with the financial advisor, it seemed that all their planning was now under threat. Cash flow problems had reached a crisis and unless Jerry's latest project won DU approval and the bonus to which that entitled him, the life plan that had driven their marriage partnership would be a cruel irrelevance.

'I have assurances from Caerleon Capital,' Jerry began, looking across his company's boardroom to his friend Nigel, 'that the equity they provide will enable us to attract investment for a leveraged buy-out of Trans Tropics by our new company Africa Enterprise. We will be able to provide attractive terms to current clients of TT, farmers who will be only too ready to exchange their share in the co-operative and the hard labour it involves for a comfortable life in the capital city. A rationalisation of labour costs will allow us to exploit the farms' ideal location six degrees north of the equator. The new company will be able to service debt and return a consistent profit to shareholders.' Jerry turned to his final slide: 'Please refer to page five showing the comparative increase in returns over the next five years' – the QED of spreadsheet and graph.

At five, hosts and guests for the dinner party that night prepare for the evening in their different ways – Jerry's game of squash with Nigel at Bannatynes has left him tired but bullish after a rare win, while on her return from Hammersmith, Brenda has made a stopover at Covent Garden, where Sorbie's Signature Facial seems to have dispelled all earlier doubts and uncertainties. They both feel confident about the outcome of tonight's dinner. Only Gordon's preparations are less auspicious as he swallows codeine and quinine to fight off shivers and a heavy sweat, and, despite the charming French girl's assurances at the stall in Borough Market, the little round box of Époisses is beginning to give off a strong odour.

Seven thirty and the through lounge of 45 Goldborne Gardens is ready for the evening. A table has been set in the window bay overlooking the playground and boating lake by Alexander Palace. A discreet arrangement of uplights has given an impression of space to the smallish room, and soon the guests are seated around a centrepiece of candles whose ochreous light brings the faces into a group bathed in chiaroscuro like the setting of a Caravaggio. Of course Brenda has contrived to create an instant intimacy between the group:- a strong scent of apple blossom room fresheners, kisses on both cheeks between guests and hosts. Nigel, the friend and business partner who has been drafted in to provide gravitas and financial heft: square-jawed, blond hair perfectly shaped from crown to nape; the effortless baritone, easy with the vowels that still mark off the country's cultural élite. Gordon, beaming with pleasure at the trouble being taken for his benefit. Jerry, nervous before his first step in takeover capitalism. Brenda, realising the long odyssey from Walsall to N10 may depend on tonight: Will Gordon accept a buyout of Trans Tropics by Africa Enterprise? And what is that bad smell tainting the fresh scent of apple blossom?

'This is make-or-break time for the African continent Dad,' says Jerry. 'With world powers competing for investment opportunities and global capital also seeking outlets for surplus funds, Africa has a once-in-life-time chance to enter the global economy on equal terms. Cheap labour, commodity and production costs give your company TT a significant advantage over its rivals. Could be a real goldmine. With a new management team recruited by my bank, IMF approval is a cert, bringing dividends to investors, financial cred to Ghana as a place of investment, while here in Britain we struggle with our problems. Just sign this document and you'll give your African partners a pay-out they had never dreamed of.'

'That's all very well,' says Gordon, 'but I was never thinking of the African continent, or the approval of the

IMF. I just wanted to give a chance to some farmers to make a go of the palm trees they had inherited from their ancestors, to give them the technological and financial knowhow to rebuild their lives and community. I never....'
But at that moment the phone rings.

'It's for you Gordon,' says Brenda. 'Some woman, sounds hysterical.' He takes the receiver.

'Is that you Gordon? Obi is very bad. Oh please help, he is very bad. Eyes red, blood from nose. And pain, so strong all over.'

Stunned and speechless, Gordon can only manage a brief 'Where are you Efua?' A moment as she asks someone and then an official voice takes over.

'I am afraid the boy is acutely ill and symptoms suggest a hemorrhagic fever. Have you been in touch with the child? Have you noticed symptoms of fever, stiffness, joint pain? Have you been in physical contact with anyone? The Emergency Protocol will require you and anyone you have been in contact with to be held in an isolation wing here at the School of Tropical Medicine.'

Sirens, anti-contamination suits, house cordoned off, horrified faces of neighbours and bystanders. Then a bare room in a building just off Gower Street. Only a few hundred yards away, Gandhi's statue in Tavistock Square and, further, in the heart of Bloomsbury, the exact spot where a number thirty bus had been destroyed by terrorists in the July 7th bombing. Now the little group is brought together sitting on benches in the isolation room, facing each other, the child fighting for his life in a specialist unit next door. Each of their private hopes and ambitions is on hold, dependent on the course of a virus which even the foremost authority of tropical diseases in the country confessed he had no way of predicting.

Brenda's mobile buzzes: 'Mummy Sam's mother's asked me to stay over another night they've got tickets for *Swan Lake* can't miss the opportunity can I oh p l e a s e? ... Mummy?

Rum and Revolution

When we land at Havana there has been a bunching of arrivals and several planeloads are being herded into a hangar-like building to form queues for immigration and customs. The boutiques and bistros of Schiphol seem a world away as we contemplate the bare walls, the ceiling festooned with flags from a hundred nations, the interminable queues. At least we are free from the consumer fantasies of the west, we say, the perfumed malls. We are a group of friends, all members of our local Labour party, anxious to experience Cuba before détente with the US brings cruise ships and capitalism: Steph, a paramedic, Caitlin a social worker and me, a retired teacher keeping busy with a little voluntary work for Citizens Advice. In Havana's Jose Marti International Airport we are learning the patience of refugees as we wait to be questioned, photographed and granted leave to enter.

The nine hour flight has left nerves frayed, but mothers, fathers, tour leaders keep spirits up with a little banter, and clothes may be rumpled but the travellers still lay claim to a certain style: culottes destined for the beaches, safari trousers for hikers, linen suits for businessmen, a baseball cap jauntily reversed, forearms blooming with tattoos. Amidst all the display I notice that one figure stands out: faded tee shirt emblazoned Year of the Rat, flip flops, aged corduroys, baggy at the knees, hanging shapeless and held up by pieces of string, a face framed by straggly beard and salt and pepper whiskers. Formalities completed, we find ourselves in the arrivals area amidst a forest of placards, one of which is for Ruskin Tours, our travel company. A short walk and we are in the little minibus that is to take us on ours, Rum and Revolution. As we wait for one last member, we look around at our fellow travellers; all seem serious-minded people, talking softly. Finally, someone trudges up the minibus steps: a faded tee shirt, Year of the Rat.

An hour later, with registration completed, the three of us gather in the atrium of the Hotel Sevilla and order our first mojitos. We savour the hotel's elegance, point out the marble floor, the vines climbing up columns, the walls with photos of old Havana, celebrities from the 40s and 50s, and listen to the little band. It has been fifteen hours since we left our local airport on our link to Amsterdam. As the saxophone keeps up a simple melody, lulled by the rhythms beaten out by drums, maracas and cowbells, we feel our eyelids begin to droop and make our way to our rooms. Passing through the reception area, I notice a familiar figure exiting the hotel into the Havana night.

At breakfast next day, we are going over guidebooks between mouthfuls of muesli when a heavily laden tray is set down on our table. The rodent shape on the tee shirt is now plain to see. Introductions completed, Roger Barton, owner of the tee shirt, takes out a circular pill dispenser and describes the simple mnemonic he has devised in case he misses a dose. As he tucks into parathas and curried omelette, more explanations, 'I always have a piece of string and flip flops for airports. Why put up with the hassle of taking off belts and shoes when you can just walk through the body scanners?'

From practicalities Roger moves on to his past life and the three of us stop eating, put down our reading matter to listen, fascinated: the nine unhappy years at a Catholic boarding school, the series of IT jobs, never quite fitting in, the trips abroad, to Bali, Sri Lanka, Thailand, alone. There is a murmur of sympathy as he ends.

We are late for the morning tour, and as we get onto the minibus, our guide Juaneta greets us with a cheery '*Date prisa mis hijos*! Hurry my children! We want to see Habana! I will show you how rum is made, how tobacco is grown. You will learn how to cut and smoke a cigar, how to dance the mambo.'

With her brown eyes and long dark hair, neat knee length black jeans, red top and pristine white trainers, with her enthusiasm and pride in her country, Juaneta seems to us the perfect guide to a resurgent Cuba. After a short drive along the Malecón we park near the Capitol Building, and she announces, 'Now, *misos ninos*, it is time to stretch our legs, or as my fellow guide so unfortunately put it, it is time to spread our legs!' We all laugh, except for Roger.

We stroll down the spacious Paseo del Prado, past the exquisite, colonnaded façade of the Gran Teatro, across the central park, to the vast expanse of the Plaza del Revolución desperately in need of its cheering crowds. At lunch the three of us find ourselves at the Museum of the Revolution, in front of a life-size sculpture of Fidel Castro flanked by Che Guevara and Camilo Cienfuegos. They seem to be in the midst of combat, Fidel's arm stretched out pointing at something, the enemy or, perhaps, the future. Che looks forward intently. The sculptor has caught the deep folds of the uniform, the stubble on his chin, the hair streaming in the wind. On his head the familiar beret that takes me back to the poster on my teenage bedroom wall. I turn to Steph and Caitlin and salute, '*Hasta la Victoria siempre*!', and we are all smiling when Roger strolls into the gallery. He stands facing Castro's outstretched arm, and for a moment I have the illusion that Fidel is pointing at him. On Roger's cheek are imprinted two full Cupid's bows in glossy red. He is unabashed when we mention this and takes out his mobile. There is a photo of a woman in a brightly coloured traditional Cuban dress, tight fitting on the hips, the skirt flared into frilly bands of boldly contrasting colours, her hair swept into an African head scarf. She is planting a kiss on his grizzled cheeks as she hides coyly behind a fan.

'Not bad for five CUCs,' he says. More trophies follow from past tours: a Balinese woman in kebaya and sarong, a white-faced geisha in a kimono, a girl from Phuket in blouse and tube skirt.

'Enough!' says Steph. 'Please excuse us. We still haven't been to the room with Fidel's attack on the Moncada Barracks.'

Later, in the cafeteria, conversation turns to Roger.

'I don't think Roger is quite on message regarding the aims of this tour,' says Steph.

'More rum than revolution,' I offer.

'Oh come on,' says Caitlin, 'don't be so hard on him. Can't you see he's lonely? He's desperately in need of contact.'

In the days that follow, other examples of Roger's behaviour begin to accumulate. His persistent lateness for the morning start is throwing Juaneta's meticulous schedule into disarray. In Trinidad, he buys a huge economy tub of ice cream which melts in the bus's refrigerator, coating everything in a sugary film, and we all have to clutch sticky water bottles as we admire the colonial style interior and furniture of the Museo Romântico. At the Che Guavara mausoleum in Santa Clara, the reverential silence is broken when Roger takes a call on his mobile from his financial advisor, and is escorted from the building by two attendants. Grumbling begins to mount and a meeting is called in his absence to discuss the problem. Only Caitlin stands up for him.

'Come on guys, cut him a little slack. Don't you see, Roger has difficulty reading other people's feelings, interpreting cues. It's not selfishness. Just be a bit more patient, make him feel secure and he'll learn how to relate.'

Then there is the incident of the land crabs. On the fourth morning we visit the museum celebrating Castro's victory over the CIA-backed invaders at the Bay of Pigs. Later, driving along the bay, we all notice a crunching sound coming from the wheels. Looking ahead we can see the road covered in red crabs trying to cross to the beach and the sea. The crunching grows louder and continuous. The road becomes a moving carpet of red. Now there is a metallic sound from one of the wheels and the minibus pulls up. A tyre has been pierced by a crab's pincer. We can see the crabs more clearly. They are large, some of them ten to twelve inches between pincers, dark red on the body, shading to lighter red claws and legs. The occasional yellow one has black and white stripes along the side of the head, deep red mandibles, an evil black eye outlined in a lighter yellow, like a pagan image of the devil. They crawl over the crushed bodies of their fellows, and once across the road some climb trees while others have covered a little shack in a bristling mantle of red. Juaneta explains that they are waiting for the right time to crawl to the waves and lay their eggs.

'Now *mis niños* it is time to spread your legs,' she continues, 'but not too wide, eh? Let us have a quick swim while we wait for the repair to our tyre.' As we leave the bus I notice Caitlin sitting rigid in her seat, her head turned away from the window.

'Bit phobic about large creepy crawlies,' she explains through gritted teeth. 'Think I'll stay in the bus.'

Stepping between the crabs, it is a relief to get away from the horror on the beach and into the warm, clear sea. I have brought my goggles and spend a few minutes watching the deep-bodied angel fish, their colours matching the pastel shades of the coral they feed on, but time is short and returning to the shore I put on my sandals when a scream rings out from the direction of the bus. I run there to find Roger standing next to Caitlin, his camera in one hand and a huge yellow crab in the other. The screaming has stopped but Caitlin has begun to hyperventilate. Her breathing becomes more rapid and her eyes have begun to roll back when Steph runs up the steps, grabs an empty beach bag and puts it over her friend's head: 'We have to build up the carbon dioxide in her system, you see.'

We are furious and turn to Roger for an explanation.

'I just wanted to take a shot of her with the crab when she started to scream... real head case.'

On the long drive to Viñales the next day the bus is unusually quiet. Caitlin has recovered, but the mood is sombre. The crab incident has somehow placed Roger beyond the pale. Juaneta is subdued, 'So many problems with this tour.' She has always gained excellent ratings as a guide, she says, and is in line for a prize from state tourism, a possible trip to London. 'But now I do not think this is likely. Something bad may happen.'

The next morning we gather on the outskirts of the little town of Viñales and look across the lush valley enclosed by the Mojotes hills, great green lozenges studding the horizon. Our walk that morning takes us through fields of cassava and tobacco. We admire the old fashioned barns for drying tobacco leaves, an ox drawing a plough, the farmers in gaucho hats riding to their fields, the village cooperatives. Horse riding is on offer and Roger books himself a two-hour slot for the afternoon. By lunchtime clouds have built up. Juaneta is worried.

'In summer the rain can be very very heavy,' she says.

But Roger is insistent. He has paid for the ride and is not going to miss it. At two o'clock, in tee shirt and shorts, he sets off with his guide. A few drops of rain have begun to fall. Within an hour the storm hits us. The rain drills down. Hours pass and the rain does not relent, subtropical rain we have never encountered. Later, when the group meets up for the evening at a restaurant overlooking the valley, we find Juaneta distraught. There has been no sign of Roger and his guide. A reddish torrent is flowing down the track towards the bottom of the valley. She arranges a search party but it finds its way blocked by a stream that has burst its banks. On her mobile she tries to contact someone with an all-terrain vehicle. Finally, at six, the rain suddenly stops. Half an hour later a figure on a horse emerges from the valley. As it approaches we can see a large white cloth over the rider's upper body. Slowly the horse makes its way up the track to the restaurant. It is Roger. He has been abandoned by his guide. One hand holds the reins, the other the edges of a white sheet a kind villager must have given the shivering foreigner. As he comes closer, we can see his hair and beard plastered down by the rain, his teeth chattering.

'He looks like Christ riding into Jerusalem,' exclaims Caitlin, and the whole group burst into cheers. It is the redemption of Roger. She welcomes him into the restaurant with a forgiving embrace.

It is our last night. Juaneta has arranged supper at El Paradiso, an organic farm run by friends, a young couple. She shares a joke with the wife who is expecting their first child. Seated at a long table on the restaurant balcony, we enjoy a relay of dishes, all produce from the farm, and look across the fertile Viñales valley to the Mojotes hills, their tops touched with red by the setting sun. Supper is to be followed by one last nightclub in the town centre. Juaneta has been teaching us the basic rhythms of Cuban dance music, and in the nightclub some of the group take to the floor trying out mambo, rhumba and danzón. There is a burst of laughter when Caitlin loses her partner attempting an ambitious turn, and a young Cuban steps in to show her the move. Soon others join in. Our whole group are dancing. The couples, Cuban and English, forget their different realities, transported by the mournful melody of the saxophone as their bodies interact in time to the salsa rhythms. Suddenly at twelve the music stops. Trumpets, saxophones, double basses, maracas are replaced by tall African drums. The dance floor is plunged in darkness and the stage is lit by a bright light. Our group moves up a little incline for a better view. I notice Roger is missing. Four drummers dressed in white begin a loud, insistent rhythm with intricate cross-beats. A female dancer in a white dress and headscarf takes to the stage. She crouches low, and a series of short, rapid steps take her across the stage where her arms shoot out and her body arcs in a gesture of pain. She is joined by a young man, also in white, a wooden rectangle about his neck and they begin to dance together. It is a story of suffering, of hard labour, cruel punishments, of men and women kept forcibly apart. The audience press closer to the stage. I fancy there is a note of anger in the applause at the end of the performance. The mood has changed and we sense hostile glances as we leave the nightclub.

In silence we make our way to our lodgings. We pass bars and restaurants still busy after midnight. The others have got a little ahead when at one corner Roger emerges from a side street. He falls into step beside me.

'You missed the performance at the end,' I say.

'Yes, saw a girl at the bar, obviously looking for business. Twenty CUCs. Wasn't going to give me the full works but I negotiated. Had to pay extra for the johnny. Bit much, don't you think? Anyway took me to a derelict old warehouse. Did the business while her friend kept watch for the police. Quite strict around here, you know. Notice the patrol on the main street?'

I am stunned. A long silence, which I begin desperately to fill with talk of our next day's departure. I am returning to England but Roger is continuing the tour to the east of the island. We discuss bus times, tipping cleaners and the bus driver, Roger oblivious of any cause for embarrassment. But his short, blunt sentences have been a shock. They seem to taint our whole experience of Cuba. Are we so different from Roger, indulging in the pleasures of the exotic and – what do they call it? – development porn, just as he has in his cruder gratifications? Back in our lodging I have a restless night, my snatches of sleep filled with vivid dreams of Roger and the dancer in the white dress and headscarf, of myself bargaining angrily with the same girl.

At breakfast next morning my friends notice how quiet I am and I find myself sharing the night's revelations.

Another silence. Then Steph exclaims: 'How sordid! Who says slavery and colonialism are over?! Western capital screws the economy, and the Western male screws the third world woman.'

'I don't know,' says Caitlin. 'He's desperately lonely. Perhaps it's the only way he can find intimacy with another person, you know, the comfort of physical contact.'

'Comfort!' scoffs Steph, 'Roger just lacks a moral compass. Something missing up here (pointing to her head).'

'That may be,' I say, 'but we have a problem. Roger had a narrow shave with the police. If he carries on like this in Santiago he's bound to get caught. Think of the disgrace to Juaneta. It could mean the end of her career.'

'Yes, we'd better do something about it. We'll have to warn her,' says Steph.

I think of Juaneta and her pride in her country, as she would tell us about its history, its customs, its vibrant music scene. I think of the young couple with the organic farm and their hopes for Cuba's future. All the youthful idealism. How could I confront her with the story of last night? I imagine the shame we would both feel. The three of us walk over to the little house where she is lodging. The landlady takes us into the room where Juaneta is having her breakfast. Her black jeans, red top and white trainers are as fresh and neat as ever, but there is a tiredness about her deep brown eyes. As they look at us they seem to sense what is coming.

The Black Boat, a Broads Mystery

A fresh north easterly caught the sails of the dinghy as she slipped out of the staithe and entered the broad itself.

'Keep the mainsheet on a close reach, Able-seaman,' said the helmsman, 'and get forward in the bows, Roger, to keep a lookout for enemy boats.'

'Aye, aye Captain,' they replied. The dinghy picked up speed across the broad to the point where it is joined by a dyke. With a shout of 'ready and about', the captain put the helm down, the crew lowered heads as the boom came across and the dinghy completed a tack. They congratulated themselves on a first successful manoeuvre, noticing as they did so a large vessel moored at the end of the dyke. It was a sea-going coaster with a deep black hull and seemed derelict but for a solar panel, a little television aerial and a row of washing on the deck. Curtains in the cabin window were carefully drawn. They tacked across the broad again and headed for the island that was their objective that day. The able-seaman turned back to look at the hulk. One of the curtains seemed to twitch.

'I think there might be pirates on that coaster, Captain,' she said.

'Well, we will have to return tomorrow and launch an attack. No time to think about enemy action now,' he replied.

They began their zig zag progress down the broad to the island, ducking the boom at each tack, leaning over the side in sudden gusts, dodging marker posts, threading their way through a flotilla of racing lasers and a windsurfer whose wake sprayed them as he completed a turn inches from their bows. At last they reached the island. Finding a gap in the reeds, Captain John steered her in and Able-seaman Titty released the halyard to lower the sail. Ship's Boy Roger made the painter good on the shore, while Mister Mate Susan dropped an anchor to secure the stern.

'I think we all deserve a tot of grog,' said Captain John, pulling out his hip flask of single malt.

'I still say we should have gone to Coniston as we always planned. It's where *Swallows and Amazons* actually took place after all,' said Titty when they sat on the bank for their first council.

'But then we were four twelve-year olds hooked on Arthur Ransome,' said Captain John, 'not a group of oldies wanting to celebrate their sixty-eighth year with the trip they'd always dreamed of. Towing a dinghy from Stevenage up the M6 at forty miles per hour to avoid overheating the trailer wheels would have exhausted us, especially Boy Roger after his coronary. We want the trip to be a celebration, not a suicide pact. Hickling Broad makes a perfect replacement for Coniston. Isn't this a good Wild Cat Island? Now stop being insubordinate Able-seaman Titty and get back into character.'

Following the detailed descriptions in *Swallows and Amazons*, the four began to set up camp. But the island provided no convenient trees between which the rope could be strung to support the pieces of cloth that formed the tents. Making do, they hung the rope between some stunted blackthorn bushes. Convenient stones to fill the side pockets of the tents to keep the walls apart were also nowhere to be found.

'Well, we'll certainly get to know one another intimately,' said Mate Susan, as they looked at the two tents, three foot high and two foot wide. 'More like a poly-tunnel than a tent. Wasn't like this in the book.'

Cooking was less of a challenge. The blackthorn bushes provided a supply of dry branches and firewood and they soon had two forked sticks driven into the ground. These supported a cross stick from which they could hang a kettle.

'I suppose I should set about preparing supper,' said Susan. 'Ransome could certainly have done with some re-education on gender roles.'

'And on the use of gender-sensitive names,' added Titty.

Susan filled the kettle from a bottle of Highland Spring, glad they hadn't relied on the dark muddy water of the broad, and lit the firewood beneath it. Soon the kettle was singing, the pemmican (eggs and sausages) sizzling in the saucepan. Spirits rose after helpings of pemmican and more tots of grog. When the summer evening turned into night they gathered together in a rendering of their favourite song,

'So we'll rant and we'll roar like true British sailors, We'll range and we'll roam over all the salt seas…'

They put out the candles in the lanterns they had hung from the bushes and made their way in the dark to their tents. In the distance they noticed a glimmer of light from the direction of the dyke, and, in the pauses of the wind, they felt sure they could hear the sound of singing.

The expedition had been anticipated for years and now at last it was taking place. The two men and two women had spent their childhood together in Stevenage in the 1970s. One of the first new towns, Stevenage had been a place of shiny glass, civic buildings in severe modernist style, all planes and verticals. The friends found it a regimented, unexciting place, and on cold, windswept weekends, their parents at the local pub, they would gather in a garage, each with well-worn copies of *Swallows and Amazons*, the paraffin heaters providing a cosy warmth and a comforting smell. They had been enchanted by the wild landscape, the freedom to lead and explore, and in the book's nautical language, with its halyards and jib-sheets, painter and thwarts, they found a sense of order, of an older England that still could be made 'shipshape'. They would act scenes from *Swallows and Amazons*, even write new ones. They would become Captain John, Able-seaman Titty, Mate Susan and Ship's Boy Roger. In the years that followed, the four continued to live in Stevenage and through marriage, children, divorce, redundancy, illness, they kept up these get-togethers, escaping into the enchanted world of their childhood. So when, in their late sixties, John got hold of an old eighteen-foot dinghy and proposed a real adventure in their own *Swallow*, they agreed, with some reservations, to humour him. After some time spent with *The Handbook of Sailing* and the YHA on line course, they felt ready to face the Broads.

Susan was the first to awake. Burrowing out of the tent, her head finally popped out to be greeted by a warm summer day. She foraged for some more firewood, and while the kettle boiled she took in the morning scene on the broad. By the far bank a group of mallards were busy at the base of some reeds, while nearer she recognised a pair of grebes by their tall necks and narrow crested heads. On a marker post a cormorant, deep black with a splash of white on its breast, kept watch like a patient waiter.

The whistle of the kettle recalled Susan to her duties. 'Come on you sluggards,' she shouted, giving gentle kicks to the shapes clearly outlined in the sides of the tents. After much grumbling, groaning, wriggling, each of the others emerged from a tent, exhausted by the effort, like an adult insect just out of its chrysalis. They sat before the fire waiting for the kettle to boil and for the slices of bread at the end of forks to toast, a phalanx of medicine bottles in front of each. When some toast had been eaten, pills swallowed with gulps of tea, and creaking limbs had become more pliant, Captain John stood up.

'Mister Mate and crew,' he said, 'I call a council.' They all looked up at him. 'We need an enemy, agreed? Now, that ugly black coaster moored at the end of the dyke, what's it up to? The crew were roistering into the early hours. Drunk the lot of them I wager, or high on drugs more like. That's it. Smuggling drugs into the country. That's what they are doing.' His eyes lit up as he imagined the triumph that would crown a moderately successful career as a Stevenage estate agent. 'With a surprise night attack we expose the drug cartel supplying East Anglia's youth with heroin.' The rest of the crew looked aghast, so he got out the chart of Hickling Broad. 'Look. A northerly's forecast, so we tack across to the west bank of the broad tonight, just below the sailing club. In the cover of darkness we paddle along the shore to this little inlet (pointing at the chart). Landing there, we can cut across the point to the black boat's mooring and surprise the crew who won't be expecting an attack from the landward side.'

'And what do we do when we have surprised them?' said Roger. 'There are only four of us, including two elderly women and one semi-invalid.'

'Details, details,' said Captain John. 'The point is something shady is definitely going on there. I propose we spend the day opposite Coots Mill, here on the map, within sight of the black boat under pretence of fishing and swimming. We observe carefully and finalise plans. Are we all agreed crew?'

'Aye, aye Captain,' they replied in a barely audible murmur.

An hour later they had arrived at Coots Mill and dropped anchor some twenty metres from a punt containing two fishermen. They set up their own rods, cast their lines and watched the floats. John took out the brass telescope and examined the black coaster at the end of Catfield Dyke. No sign of life. A traditional, gaff-rigged cruiser sailed past them. Then a Cornish Shrimper. Time passed. Still no movement on the black boat. John then examined the fishermen's punt more carefully with the telescope. The two men were dressed in camouflage army jackets and trousers, beanies to match. He noted one heavy pike rod, a lighter rod for catching bait fish, and two huge landing nets.

'Those natives are serious fishermen,' he said, passing the telescope to Titty. She took in the fishermen and then turned the telescope to the shore to examine the mill. Next to the mill she noticed a khaki Land Rover. It was covered with insignia and messages: there were several black eagles with wings outstretched, heads turned to the right; a ring surrounding the cross of St. George; a large C18 in white sprayed on the bonnet; messages in black gothic script – 'Make England safe,' 'England, love it or leave it,' 'Born in England, Live in England, Die in England'.

'That must be the fishermen's Land Rover,' said Titty, passing the telescope to John, 'do you want to take a look?' John examined the vehicle carefully, puzzled by the unfamiliar insignia, but Titty had come across sentiments like those of the fishermen in her years as a social worker in Stevenage.

One o'clock. Still no sign of life from the black boat. The July sun was now high in the sky and the breeze had fallen, making the cramped dinghy an uncomfortable place.

'Time for that swim,' said Captain John, 'it will refresh us all.' The others looked at the still, black water and made their excuses, but John was not to be discouraged and taking up position on the stern deck, he jumped in. Unimpeded for the first metre or so, his feet then met something soft into which they sank deeply, releasing gases that had built up after years of putrefaction. As he resurfaced a powerful stench rose up over the dinghy, causing the crew to turn away in disgust. By now John had created some interest from passing holiday cruisers, and to reassure them he began a front crawl. After circling a few times he returned to *Swallow* to get out, but the gunwales were at least two feet above the water and his attempt to pull himself into the dinghy was a failure. Boy Roger was excused because of his medical condition, and so Titty and Susan each took one of John's arms, and attempted to haul him in. Several times they managed to get his head up to the edge of the gunwale, but then he would fall back

It had now become urgent to extricate John from Hickling Broad, and putting reservations aside, Titty called out to the fishermen for help. They quickly reeled in their lines, stowed their rods and rowed over to *Swallow*.

'No probs chaps, we've landed pike nearly as big as this,' the younger one said. 'If he gets into a crouching position, we'll get the two landing nets under his bum and, as we lift, if you could give a haul on his arms, we should manage to get him in.' They made one last effort. This time Boy Roger helped too because of the gravity of the situation. Finally the Captain was safely landed in the bottom of the boat. Titty and Susan fell back exhausted. Boy Roger's face had gone white with the effort. For several minutes Captain John lay gasping, much like a pike landed by one of the fishermen. Finally he raised his head and mumbled a few words of thanks.

'Don't worry mate,' said Mark, 'it give us a chance to try out some of the skills we learned at camp.' John looked puzzled. 'You know, combat training. Got to keep the ol' country safe haven't we?'

'Yes, yes, keep the ol' country safe. Marvellous,' said John, and, looking at Titty, 'great lads aren't they?' But before she could reply, John noticed a thin wisp of smoke rising out of the funnel of the black boat.

'Smugglers!' he shouted, grabbing the telescope, and began to study the boat intently. He explained his theory about drug smuggling to the two fishermen and the plan to board the boat that night.

'There's certainly something being smuggled,' said Mark, the older fisherman, and Titty noticed the look he gave his mate Jason when he added, 'Good luck tonight. You be careful, mind.'

Back on Wild Cat Island, it was clear that the black boat had become an obsession with John. He talked of nothing else on the return sail and at supper around the camp fire there was talk of arming themselves for an assault with willow withies cut from the trees by Coots Mill. The rim of one of the landing nets had damaged a tendon behind his knee, and, his face haggard and tense, he limped about the camp, finding fault with everyone. He shouted at Titty when he found her using her mobile secretly behind a blackthorn bush, a grave breach of rules. He accused her of fomenting mutiny when he caught her whispering with Susan by their tent. No longer was he the calm, collegiate Captain John of *Swallows and Amazons*, ready to take advice, showing practical common sense. He was Captain Ahab, striding about on his whale bone stump, driven mad by the pursuit of the white whale, or in John's case by the pursuit of the black boat. As they went over plans for the night's mission, he became impatient with their demand for more detail.

'It is a great mistake,' he said, 'to make very detailed plans. As Von Moltke said, no battle plans survive contact with the enemy.'

'Or, as Mike Tyson put it,' offered Roger, 'everyone has a plan until they get punched in the mouth.'

'Exactly,' said John. 'Best not to be hampered by detailed plans, but to improvise and respond to a situation as it develops.'

So, as the last rays of the July sun began to fade, they set out on their mission. They sailed up the broad until the light had gone completely; then they lowered the main sail and began to paddle towards the point where the dyke enters the broad. They guided *Swallow* into the bank, stowed their paddles, and crossed the narrow headland to where the black boat was moored. The singing was now loud and clear. It was in a foreign language, but it was no roistering song. The mournful melody evoked a deep sadness, a longing for someone or some place lost forever.

'I'll enter the coaster first and get the savages into conversation,' whispered John, his voice tense with excitement. 'When they let down their guard, I'll shout 'Swallows!' and the three of you rush in. Overcome with shock, they will agree to our terms and hand over the contraband drugs. We can then escort them to a police station.'

Alarmed by the vagueness of these plans, the crew were about to protest, but John, high on adrenalin, had jumped onto the coaster. His shoes rang out loud as he landed on the metal deck. The singing stopped. There was some movement below as he limped across the deck and disappeared down the hatch. The others waited for his call. There was the sound of a struggle, of objects being knocked over, some grunting, and finally a muffled 'Swallows!' The three ran across the deck and down the hatch, to find Captain John expertly trussed and tied to the stanchion in the main cabin. There were two men of Middle Eastern appearance standing on either side of him. The older of them spoke.

'What are all you people doing down here? We no want trouble.' At that moment, the metal deck rang out again as more bodies landed on it. Two figures came down the steps to the cabin. Mark and Jason.

'Captain John! Looks like we've got to rescue you again. We'll be having to claim salvage next time!' said Jason, gesturing to the two foreigners to release John. They were no match for the tall, burly Englishmen with the long hunting knives in their hands. By the time John was free, two young women in burkas and two children had appeared from one of the inner cabins.

'Smuggling drugs!' Mark scoffed, 'this is much more precious contraband.'

'Yeah,' said Jason, 'we've been keeping an eye on the coaster for the last week, ever since we heard that a boat had arrived here from Yarmouth. When you told us about your plans, we thought we'd better act tonight and forget about the rest of the gang.'

'Gang?' said John.

'People smugglers. We'll take this lot to Yarl's Wood. You could do us a good turn here, seeing as we've helped you out. There's only room for the two men in our punt. It'd be great if you could take the women and children in your dinghy to Coots Mill where the Land Rover's parked.'

By now the children and the two women were crying. John was deeply moved by the sight, but the right, responsible thing to do was to help the Englishmen.

'Yes, yes, of course we will,' he said.

What happened next took only a few seconds, but they were to be the most momentous seconds in the lives of *Swallow's* crew. Jason handed his knife to Titty.

'Here, take this, love, while I frisk them,' he said, and then, his tone suddenly different, 'you never know what the bitches might be hiding.' He began to search one of them, his hands lingering over her breasts and thighs. 'Cor, Mark, wouldn't mind a couple of hours in my tent with this one, eh?' The woman turned aside in shame, and as she did so, one of the men sprang forward and grabbed Jason's arms. In a moment Jason had him by the throat.

'No you don't mate. That was one big mistake. I can now claim self-defence.' He began to throttle the man. A knife flashed. The other woman had hidden a knife in the sleeves of her burka and now drove its blade deep into Jason's back. He turned and looked at her in surprise before sinking to the floor.

'Jason!' said Mark and then turned to the woman, raising his knife, 'Why, you sneaking…!' As he lifted his arm to strike, Titty had an instant to decide. Something took over, instinct, reflex, a fellow feeling for a woman insulted and about to be killed. A sudden thrust and she had stabbed Mark in the stomach. He too fell to the floor, blood pouring from the wound. Titty knelt by him, and, now wanting to be his saviour, tried to stanch the flow of blood.

'Hold on, Mark!' she said. 'We'll phone for an ambulance.' The knife had severed an artery. He looked questioningly at Titty, but then his eyes glazed over. She looked in horror at her blood-covered hands, then to where Susan was kneeling over Jason and to where the children clung to their mothers for comfort.

'Jason's dead,' said Susan.

The knife had passed between his ribs and into his heart.

John had witnessed the scene in disbelief. He had not moved or spoken. Swallows, Amazons, natives, pirates, savages, the words fell away from him together with the certainties they represented. Finally, he began, 'We'd better….'

But Susan interrupted, 'Nothing we can do for these two, let's get the others out of here.'

Authority had also fallen away from John, as Susan and Titty took control of the situation. The scene inside the boat was arranged to suggest a fight had taken place between Jason and Mark, knives placed in their hands. An anonymous phone call would, later, bring the police to the black boat. The four adults and two children were taken onto *Swallow*. Titty turned to look at the black coaster and noticed that a large C18 had been sprayed onto the side in luminous white paint. Then, low in the water with the extra weight, the dinghy was paddled slowly to The Pleasure Boat. The pub, though empty, was lit up and clearly visible in the night. They were able to find a free mooring at the staithe, and Titty carefully guided the dinghy in. Roger made good the painter on one of the posts, and crew and passengers disembarked. A young man approached from The Pleasure Boat car park.

'Hello Tommy,' said Titty, embracing the young man.

'Hello Mum, I'll take over now,' her son replied. 'The minibus is waiting in the car park. After you phoned I contacted our network and they knew all about the black boat in Hickling Broad.'

'What can they do for them?'

'Arrange safe houses. Just think what they have been through. There's a lot of sympathy for asylum seekers from Idlib at the moment and our lawyers should manage to get them all refugee status.' He paused for a moment. 'And Mum, you've been marvellous. If it hadn't been for your hunch about the black boat, and your phone call, these two families might have been sent back to Syria and probable death.' He paused again and then, whispering, 'And Mum, what about... 'Captain John'? Any further deterioration? Be honest now.' A grimace of pain before she nodded slowly. Tommy continued, 'The three of you have been wonderful friends to him but it's time you all faced the truth about his condition. Behaviour more and more erratic ...dangerous even like tonight. Time to think about permanent care for the old boy?' Tommy then went over to the Syrians and spoke to them in what sounded like Arabic and they all walked slowly over to the car park.

The crew of *Swallow* could not bring themselves to talk about what had happened, the enormity of it. There was no need to hold any council. They all knew what they had to do and set about it with barely a word spoken. They reassumed their Stevenage identities. A favourable wind took them back to their island and after a sleepless night, and a rushed breakfast next morning, they struck camp. In silence they sailed back to the staithe in Hickling. In silence they lifted *Swallow* onto the trailer, and in silence they loaded their baggage in the car. Not until they reached Newmarket was the silence broken.

'In naval warfare, two things are important,' said Captain John, resuming command, as he kept the Volvo and its trailer at a steady 40mph, 'to know exactly what you want to do and to do it in the manner that your enemy least expects. The wind will be from the north tomorrow, so the Amazons are sure to attack us.'

'I don't see how we are going to catch *Amazon* if they come here in her,' said Susan, a touch of weariness in her voice.

'I have a plan for that,' said Captain John. 'If there's a northerly wind, one of us takes *Swallow* and hides her in the reeds...'

And so the crew of *Swallow* performed their favourite adventure, the battle between the Swallows and the Amazons. Each member of the crew knew exactly what to say, think and feel. As the car and trailer entered the outskirts of Stevenage they had reached the point in the adventure where the crew celebrates victory with tots of grog and their favourite song.

'So we'll rant and we'll roar like true British sailors,
We'll range and we'll roam over all the salt seas, ...'

They would enjoy other *Swallows and Amazons* reunions, but they never went back to Hickling Broad and never once referred to what had happened in the black boat. Not even when they read the headline in their daily paper, **The Hickling Murders. A Combat 18 Feud, say Police!**

Gender Trouble/Gender Troubled

At Seraglio, a Turkish café a few hundred yards from the university, a scattering of coffee drinkers was quietly catching up on *The New Left Review*, *Economist*, and *Times Higher*, while a noisier group had seated itself in an alcove by the bookshelves discussing the nine o'clock lecture, second in the series Transgressive Sexualities by Doctor Barry Barraclough, specialist in TS, and in transgression generally. The course had seemed a bit of a joke to the four mature students, housewives and mothers all, and perhaps there had been a touch of adventure, even rebellion. The lecture that morning had dealt with one of the mid-twentieth century French erotic classics.

'Sorry Cara, but I just can't do with it at 9 a.m. on a wet Monday morning. And probably not at any time at all. Certainly not after having to scrabble around for a red-nose day costume for Jade and then forgetting to pack Dan's Huggies – another humiliation at Tunstall Tots! I don't want to hear about a French aristocrat licking every inch of his mistress's body in a taxi driving around Marseilles.'

'But Jenny you must admire the Frenchman's style,' said Cara, 'his casual flic of the embroidered garters, the sheer technical know-how as he unhooked the corset, the care with which the lace camisole was draped over the taxi fare metre. My Jason would probably have had to call in the AA for help.'

'I suppose you have to recognize the writer's courage way back in 50s France,' said Jenny, '"the first woman to recognize female desire, in all its perverseness" and all that. Still why did Barry have to use such a crappy translation. I found the female geography difficult to follow, especially in his Midlands accent. What with womb instead of fanny, seeds instead of semen, lips and cracks between legs and bootucks, pelts of fur proudly surmounting the 'muns veneris', it was all very disorientating.'

In the group of four young women, there were two who had not spoken: 'But it was the way he read the passage, slow, deliberate, his eyes boring straight through me,' said romantic Alice dreamily.

'I wish he would bore straight through me, his ginger moustache tickling my cheeks,' said Sophie, the most adventurous of the four.

'What! Little Legs?!' said Cara. 'His whiskers wouldn't reach your navel Sophie.'

'But it's these small men who are a bundle of sexual energy,' she countered. 'There's a long line of them in history, Napoleon, Putin, Sarkozy, and who was the one with the scooter and croissants?... Oh yes, Hollandais.'

'I think you mean Francois Hollande,' said Jenny.

The four liked the scrubbed wood tables of Seraglio, its miscellaneous chairs and sofas, wall décor of political slogans, framed coffee sacks on the wall, the rows of strange liquors, Curaçao, Nagpur Old Raj Gin, and the prints, of McQueen, *Absinthe a La Mort*, *Portrait of Ira*, Sophie Dahl in the advert for Opium. It was so much nicer though less convenient than the scrubbed plastic and bright, gloss-painted walls of the uni cafeteria. And of course it had proper coffee, beans from Nicaragua. It was the Opium advertisement they turned their attention to now.

'It's exploitation!' said Jenny. 'All the old sexist imagery is still there, legs apart, back arched, head thrown back and mouth open in ecstasy, the virginal white skin, set against luxurious black velvet, the red lips and hair, hints of the scarlet woman. All the old stereotypes. Woman as object of the male gaze, passive object for man's pleasure.'

'But it's not passive, that's the point,' argued Cara. 'This is a woman who is asserting **her** right to pleasure, to violate taboos. And what's more, this is a real woman, with fleshy stomach and curves, not some anorexic waif, like Schiffer or poor Georgina Wilkin. This is the face that launched a million sexy selfies. It's the image that changed the history of the female body, gave ordinary women with ordinary bodies the right to sexual narcissism.'

'Still, I don't see any age lines or stretch marks, and she is still adopting the usual pose of surrender.'

'Well perhaps that's what women want. It's surely up to them to decide.'

'Who knows what women want, as someone or other so perceptively said. You're obviously sold on all this porno-chic Cara. Still I'd better get off, got to do some shopping at Lidl and grab a sandwich if I'm going to make Barry's seminar this aft. See you later.'

The afternoon seminar was on 'Capitalism, Pornography and the Development of Contemporary Fiction'. Doctor Barraclough had re-arranged the rows of desks in Room 2-14 to form a small square. Dressed in his signature black biker's jacket, crisp white shirt and Levi 501s, he had seated himself to one side, on a desk looking down on the group from Seraglio. Following his usual practice, Barraclough began by reading an extract from that afternoon's text. Without the anonymity of the lecture audience that morning, unable to make surreptitious checks on text messages or whispered comment to neighbour, the group of four found the atmosphere intimidating. It was a gloomy winter afternoon and every thirty seconds Barraclough would raise an extended arm to keep the motion sensitive lights on. Gone was the Gallic elegance, the exquisite aristocratic manners of the morning's extract. The vocabulary was blunt Anglo-Saxon or sex manual, D.H. Lawrence meets Cosmopolitan. It was a scene between a male client and two female escorts who were indistinguishable in name, appearance and personality, narrated in the neutral tone of a jaded reporter describing an angling competition. Without the right of choice or the possibility of resistance, the fictional women's yielding lacked the frisson of a genuine seduction. Androids programmed to perform, their submission was no more erotic than a grotesque game of 'Simon says do this'. Genitalia and other parts, male and female, were treated in isolation from body or person for purposes of pleasuring. They were rubbed, penetrated, smelled, licked, tasted and finally devoured. Climaxes followed climaxes until they became anti-climaxes. Sensation followed sensation, leaving the male narrator unsatisfied. Consumption needed some surplus and excess, and so body parts became literally isolated, dismembered, the decapitated head of one of the girls being used by the client to reach a ghoulish orgasm.

At this point there was a moan of revulsion from one of the mature students. With nine childbirths between them, they had nevertheless found the explicitness and obsessive anatomical detail acutely embarrassing. Heads looking down on their texts in shame, they all blushed to the roots of their hair. Noticing his audience's reaction, Barraclough began his commentary.

'I see embarrassment, shame, that's good. Taboos have been transgressed. We think of our age as one of sexual liberation. Freud, Masters, Kinsey, Comfort, sex therapy available in our morning newspaper together with our toast and coffee. Language has seemingly penetrated every area of erotic experience labelling, categorising, normalising, bringing the polymorphous forms of human sexuality under its control: onanism, paederasty, scopophilia, necrophilia. How can we escape from this regime of control except in moments of disgust, revulsion – in passages like this one where the limits of acceptable speech are broken? Girls, you do see that don't you? And yes Jenny it is disturbing, the narrator's consumption of pleasure after pleasure, a sort of carnal bulimia. But remember this is a satire of Wall Street in the 1980s, a gross parody of mass consumerism and liberal capitalism in Reagan's America. The hero's consumption of sexual experiences is simply the counterpart...'

And so it went on, the four housewives making notes in their folders, until, finally, with a last salute, Barraclough brought the session to an end, 'Remember, we start our case study next week, Cynthia Payne, Dominatrix to the Non-Doms.'

It was a subdued group that met in Seraglio after the seminar. In joining the course, they knew they had signed up to something edgy, something that would take them out of their comfort zone, but they all felt there had been something wrong about the afternoon session.

'It was the way he seemed to enjoy our embarrassment,' said Jenny, 'rubbing our faces in the spectacle of women being degraded, their bodies cut up and played with, lingering over every bit of filth and gore. It was like a violation. Well I'm not going to be subjected. Here's to Potteries Pussy Riot,' and they all took a deep draught of the house red that had been brought to their table. The wine worked its magic and soon they were all their usual, confident, feisty selves.

'All that anger, where did it come from,' said romantic Alice. 'Probably neglected as a baby. Needs a good cuddle.'

'Needs a good shag!' said adventurous Sophie. 'Obsessed with sex. A good shag would get it out of his system.'

'Oh yes and we know who'd provide it,' said Cara. 'Seriously though, what can we do about it? Have we got to put up with him sat up there above us, telling us what to think, confronting us with pudenda like a sophisticated sort of exhibitionist? No, I don't think so. I'm going to stop it.'

Later, Cara spent the evening going over some of the feminist classics again, De Beauvoir, Dworkin, Millet, Greer, Cixous. She wanted to challenge Barraclough intellectually and needed to be sure of her ground. But there were other strategies she could deploy too, and by the end of the evening she had developed a plan. The next morning she approached Barraclough and asked for an appointment to discuss concerns she had about the course.

'Look here Cara, why not pop over to my flat this evening. Let's talk it through over a nice glass of Rioja. I'm sure I can sort out your problems for you.' Delivered with a knowing smile on the lecturer's face, the invitation had been delivered as a challenge. Clara accepted and times were agreed, address and directions given.

After lectures that day Barraclough made his way back to his flat in a lighter mood than usual, buoyed by the possibilities of the evening to come. Colleagues had always commented on the anomaly of his apartment being situated over a florists, his 'fuck-pad', as they called it, just a few feet above the cloying sentimentality of 'Blooming Burslem'. With Valentine's Day just a week away, there were hearts made out of blood red roses set on a background of white carnations, pink tulips and pale narcissi married with roses and germini in the 'Pure Romance Bouquet', and the individualised messages, 'Fifty Years, Vera, My Love Still Smelling of Roses'. Taking in the familiar sugar rush of scent and colour, deploring this world of cliché, Barraclough walked through the shop and up the stairs to his flat. The décor of the sitting room was minimalist retro. The centrepiece a couch in faux-zebra skin, floorboards painted black with a thick pile white rug in front of a mock fifties gas fire. In one corner a juke box and on the McIntosh teak sideboard along one wall his collection of five lava lamps. Life size posters of Brando and Monroe on another wall and, dotted about, prints that bore witness to his academic specialism.

A shower followed by a liberal splashing of L'Uomo for Men found him looking at the mirror, trimming his moustache, girding his loins for the evening encounter. 'Some bird's goin' to get lucky tonight.' He smiled at his own quotation from *Kes*. He put on his favourite Sonny Terry and Brownie McGhee number, lit some joss sticks and sat in front of the five lamps, admiring the curvaceous shapes, the cyclical release of soft globes, brooding on the eternal feminine. 'You've got bad blood baby and I think you need a shot,' he hummed, when a knock at the door distracted him from the row of lava lamps. It was Cara.

'Welcome,' he said, taking her coat, and, noticing her survey of the room, continued, 'come and view my little collection before we... get down to business.' They walked past the prints. 'Goya's *Naked Maja*, such dignity don't you think? And Fuseli's *The Nightmare*, some erotic dream eh? Here's a rather naughty series of vignettes by von Bayros. And lastly of course, Courbet's *L'Origine du monde*.'

Cara winced at the exposure, the vulnerability of Courbet's female model. But the little tour had had the opposite effect to what Barraclough intended and, undaunted, she sat down on one of the Ercol chairs. She began the speech she had prepared: 'Doctor Barraclough, I can't understand how you can defend that passage we studied yesterday. It was pure pornography: <u>porno graphy</u>, Greek words meaning the depiction of women as vile whores; it turns women into objects available for male violence, rape.'

'But Cara, don't you see that pornography has been the term used by a male elite to conceal from women and the lower classes images of bodies and behaviour the elite considered anarchic, a threat to the social order. To keep those images hidden away in secret men-only collections. If it is so degrading to women how do you explain that a million mostly female readers have recently enjoyed a book by a woman describing how a woman has willingly allowed herself to be manacled and subjected to sexual violence – for her own pleasure?'

'But it all depends on the situation doesn't it?' responded Cara. 'Those women freely chose to read about some unusual kinds of sex, and apparently got a thrill from it. It was a woman writing and the woman in the novel voluntarily entered into the relationship. Yesterday it was you, a privileged male, forcing a group of women to listen to him reading about the grotesque degradation of women. The power relations were quite different.'

'Look here, Cara, why don't you leave that uncomfortable chair and join me on the sofa, where we can explore those power relations further?'

At this point there was a knock and Cara jumped up to open the door. It was Jenny. Transformed. In black leather jacket, white shirt and Levi's. With her auburn hair and a moustache from Aladdin's Cave, the resemblance to Barraclough was uncanny.

'You really need a kiss,' said Cara, caught Jenny by the waist, bent her over backwards and delivered a long passionate kiss. It was Rhett and Scarlett in *Gone with the Wind*, except that the kiss and line were delivered by Vivienne Leigh and it was Clark Gable who leant back in passive submission. Cara turned to Barraclough: 'For all your talk of transgression, Barry, you're still trapped in the old stereotypes: male/female, dominance/passivity, violator/victim, all those dreary oppositions. You need to go beyond them, reverse them, play with them, enjoy the multiple identities we're all capable of. And for a start you can get rid of those ridiculous lamps.' Cara picked up her coat, took Jenny by the arm and marched out.

Barraclough was stunned. It had been like looking in a mirror. Himself and yet not himself. The self he had so carefully nurtured, tough guy intellectual, the Brian Cox of Media Studies, a mistress in every Northern campus, two thousand followers on twitter, had it all been an act, a performance? The persona that seemed to fit him like his own skin, just a costume, moustache and a few props? Were there other selves he could inhabit? Questions plagued him through a sleepless night, and he awoke, shaken and disorientated. Still in a dream he stumbled down the stairs to the day's lectures. But, unusually, he lingered in Blooming Burslem, admiring the creations: scarlet Peruvian lilies, white lilacs and chrysanthemums framed by baby's breath, succulent purple and pale green flowers of hellebore and vivid yellow mahonia set against leaves of dogwood. Finally he approached the shop counter: 'One Pure Romance Bouquet please'.

'Certainly Sir, would that be in the pink or blue wrapping paper?'

At the Cauld Pool

In one smooth movement the salmon rod sketches a figure of eight in the air, before, drawn to one side, it drags the heavy line, ripping the water's surface, back behind the fisherman. A pause, and then a thrust of the rod shoots line and trace and fly across the stream, where they hover a moment before falling gently to the waves. A dark silhouette on the river bank, the fisherman takes a pace or two after every cast to cover likely lies, each head and tail of rapids, each long slow glide, each dark, deep pool. The fly nudges around rocks, swirls in eddies, hangs in the slower water, until, feeling the pull of the line, it skates to the side. At a little distance, a heron wading in the shallows peers for fry, while further along the river a goosander leads her brood of five, her small, sleek, tufted head erect.

From the door of the fishing hut a man is watching the scene through binoculars. For Colin Baker there has always been something about the Tweed, the very names – Kelso, Hawick, Dryburgh, Sir Walter Scott at Abbotsford, the Junction Pool where Tweed and Teviot meet, with Floors Castle on its rise of green beneath a horizon of trees. Already, there has been an evening at the hotel where deep in an armchair on the faded tartan carpet, by an empty fireplace, he listened to an old fisherman talk of ghillies, gaffs, grilse, spring and autumn runs and flies, Jack Scott, Toppy, Meg with the Muckle Mouth..., all to lure salmon. King of fish.

Later, in his room, he read of William Scrope fishing the Junction Pool in the eighteen twenties, how a voracious fish made a dash for his fly and was away like a rocket as the reel sang and fifty, then a hundred yards of line shot out. How it dragged Scrope through rapids, an arch of Melrose bridge, how he followed, floundering on dry land through alder bushes, wading through shallows, panting, exhausted. A shout to the boy to get the boat ready, and they rowed as the fish, still on the line, sought the sea. Until, in the wide, deep Cauld Pool it began to tire. One last rush when the fish saw the raised leister, the five-pronged spear, before it was finally despatched. Scrope had been dragged a mile and three quarters by the salmon in a struggle lasting several hours.

That was two hundred years ago, not far from where Colin now watches. In the bothy, the fishing hut, he is fitted out in waders, boots and salmon rod, and on the bank Finn the ghillie explains how to read the river, how salmon sit near the faster flows, in the oxygenated water. He demonstrates the casts, the roll, the single and double Spey. Finn is in a hurry, as later that morning he expects a party of Russians. After a few practice casts, Colin settles into an easy rhythm: cast, wait, watch, retrieve, pause, thrust. The dark hackle of the fly makes its mazy way, riding high in the slower water, doused in rapids, skirting boulders, at times barely visible in the dazzling bars of sunlight deflected from the water's surface. For Colin every snag, every dip of the fly is a salmon. He can almost see the swirl of its tail, almost feel its pull. There, in the deep pool under the alders it must lie. To reach it he must wade, inching forward, his feet slipping on the boulders. The water rises to his waist, to his chest. He feels the power of the current. And what if he were to hook a monster? He remembers the body of the drowned fisherman carried twenty five miles downstream from Peebles, and the stories, 'Thae that the Kelpie grips seldom rise again'.

He is totally absorbed and at first has not heard the barking, but it is closer now and he turns to see a youth throwing stones into the river for a large dog. There is a girl with him. The dog, greyhound-shaped, with shaggy white hair, chases the stones into the shallows, then stops and starts to bark and whine. Colin knows it is hopeless now, the fish are gone, but carries on regardless, until the youth and his dog are barely twenty paces from him. He turns accusingly.

'You got a problem mate?' says the youth, swinging the dog's chain in his hand. Colin notes the tight black jeans and brilliant white trainers, the muscular arms in a black short-sleeved tee shirt. He feels the contrast with his own khaki waders and fishing gilet, his protective goggles and tweed flat cap.

'It's the salmon, you see, you've frightened them off with all the splashing and the noise.'

'You what?' says the youth. 'Hoity toity English twat. Right honourable Tightarse, you don't own Scotland anymore, yer know. Fuck off to Chelsea, Hampstead, or wherever.' Then, turning to the girl with him, 'Silly old bawbag, with his face like a well-skelped arse.' In a burst of laughter they both walk on, with the dog bounding ahead of them.

'Time for a wee dram?' says Finn, who has witnessed the scene and hurried to the side of his client.

'Dinna fash yersel wi' that eediot,' he says back in the bothy as he pours whisky into two tumblers. 'Toffs in four-wheel drives, that's what they call salmon fishers, and folk like me lackeys of the old gentry. Why bother about salmon rivers when your fish farms bring in a cool billion? No matter the sea lice they spread killing the wild fish.' He describes how the lice parasite devours the fish's protective layer of mucus, bores deeper, feeding vampirically on its blood. As he listens, Colin begins to share Finn's passion, to see the playful seal pup with its big brown eyes as a predator, decimating salmon stocks. To cull the pups no longer seems taboo. Picture-perfect heron, goosander? Bellies full of young salmon, should be shot. He finishes his whisky and gets up to inspect the bothy's memorabilia: vintage fishing rods, gaffs, photos – tweed-suited squires displaying the day's catch of ten or twenty salmon laid out on the grass, a ghillie leaning on his staff. As he leaves the hut, a Land Rover pulls up. It must be the Russian party. Two men, father and son perhaps, immaculate in grey jackets zipped to the chin, dark glasses, get out, followed by a young woman in jeans and tee shirt. She collects a hamper from the boot and the group enter the hut.

Back at the river, Colin fishes the Cauld Pool, hopes buoyed by the whisky, but as the sun rises in the sky his arms begin to ache and his attention wanders – to the bronze metallic glint of a dragonfly's long body, a cluster of golden dung flies on a cowpat, its rich smell. It gets hot under the gilet and waders and he is grateful for the soothing flow of cool water he can feel through the rubber. He tries one last cast before a break for sandwiches and coffee. There is the merest ruffle of the water's surface as the fly disappears and he feels a quivering at the end of the rod. No monster then. A lift of the rod brings a wriggling five-inch strip of silver from the water, a young salmon that has changed its livery of dark blue bars and pink mottling for the silver scales that will dazzle predators at sea. The man removes the hook. Difficult to believe that the little body will spend years in the seas off Norway or Greenland, that in the small, narrow head is imprinted a memory that will lead it back to the river where it was spawned.

As he carefully releases the fish in the water, Colin hears a repressed giggle behind him. It is the woman from the Russian party, holding her sides, pressing lips together until a snort and then a guffaw break the noon stillness.

'Such a big rod,' she says, 'so much equipment, for such a little fish! My brothers and I used to catch fish so big,' holding her hands wide. 'The Kharlovka, that is a river, deep, fast-flowing rapids, you know. Very dangerous. Plenty people drowned. Not like this... little stream. No big fish here I think. But good for swimming eh?'

With that, she takes off her clothes and runs into the pool, oblivious of stones and boulders. In the middle she ducks down, her white body barred by the dark bands of underwear visible in the clear water. She breaks the surface, laughing.

'It's lovely. You should try.'

The man is about to answer when a large dog rushes past him into the shallows, barking at the woman. She laughs, 'Oh, is a Borzoi, like Mishka my dog back home,' and paddling to the side she starts to play with it. 'Your dog?' she says to the youth as he and his girlfriend walk up, and when he nods, 'He's lovely. You are so lucky to have him.'

'Oh ay, he's a grand fella, but a bit of a dafty as you can see.'

Back on the bank, the dog shakes itself spraying them, and they all laugh. The girlfriend sees that the Russian woman is beginning to shiver and takes off her sweatshirt to offer it as a towel.

Colin slips away from the group and trudges back to the hut, from which Finn and the Russians have yet to appear. Placing his rod on the frame outside, he opens the hut door to meet thick tobacco smoke and sees a table littered with the remains of a meal. There are salami rolls, glazed sausages, jars of paté, hunks of baguette and a bottle of single malt next to different brands of vodka. Finn and the Russians, shirts open at the neck, are arguing loudly. Barely noticed, he makes his way to a dark corner to take off his waders.

'Canna you see?' says Finn, his face flushed. 'It's no possible. No salmon to be removed before the end of June. It's only the 20th today. All catches ha' to be released. What's not to understand?'

'But all this money I have paid,' says the older man, 'you mean I cannot take even one big fish home tonight?'

'You see his wife will mock him,' says the younger, laughing, 'if he spend the whole day fishing and no fish.'

''Fraid it'll ha' to be a trip to the fishmonger then,' says Finn.

The Russian takes a wad of notes from his pocket and starts placing them, one by one, in front of Finn. Embarrassed, Colin hangs his waders on a peg and, with a nod to Finn, leaves the hut, finished with fishing for the day.

Later that evening he is looking out of his hotel window at the lawn sloping down to the river Tweed. Beneath a pergola covered with yellow roses, there are guests at a corporate function holding champagne glasses and talking loudly. They barely glance at the river, at the Junction Pool, where two rivers meet and salmon gather on their way to the spawning grounds. It costs six hundred pounds a day to fish there. Colin leaves the window and, on his bed, begins to read another book borrowed from the hotel: 'Ah me! I can see Sir Walter now throw his line wi' a 16lb rod across the Cauld Pool and make her licht like a feather on the other side....'

The Offering

Tommy Chisholm slept in a little corner room of the top floor apartment his parents rented in a mansion in Ballygunge, then a leafy suburb of Calcutta. One window overlooked a huge peepal tree, its massed leaves hiding the succulent figs beloved of little birds. The other gave onto a small part of the garden belonging to ground floor tenants, a rectangle laid out in mossy stone slabs with ornamental shrubs and sculptures of Indian deities. A shady space, cool on the hottest days, it was lit up by the fiery colours of a macaw which had pride of place on a stand, where with its gunmetal beak it would tear apart the fruit and nuts that appeared every day on a little tray. Sometimes Tommy would gaze at the peepal tree and the heart-shaped leaves that moved ceaselessly even on windless days. Sometimes he would look down on the little garden, alluring in its cool elegance but guarded by the bird and its fearsome bite.

His parents' own share of the garden was much larger, with a tennis court lawn, and always, it seemed, in bright sunlight. On two sides there were lines of shrubs and smallish trees, and, opposite the house, beds of cannas and dahlias enclosed by a long wall. Beyond the wall was a wilderness of tangled thorns and further still in the distance could be seen the dhobis, beating shirts and sheets on flat stones surrounding a little lake. Tommy enjoyed the freedom of the garden, from the main gate to the long wall, playing football barefoot with Chabila and the other children or hunting lizards with a catapult made from a tree branch and rubber strips cut from an old inner tube. He was ruthless in the hunt, pursuing his prey from tree to tree until it fell to the ground disfigured by blood and gore. A frangipani tree gave convenient access to the wall, its many low branches seeming to offer an easy climb, but the soft wood was deceptive and broke easily, a poisonous milky liquid oozing from the wound. Tommy would lead his friends along the wall, beating the bounds of their little kingdom and looking down on the tangle of thorns, infested by *saanp*, snakes, warned Laloo, the bearer. School was weekdays eight to one. That left the afternoons and weekends for Tommy to run free in the garden with the other children, a cotton wool bandage around his neck in a fruitless attempt to ward off the bouts of tonsillitis which often sent him to bed with a temperature.

It was rare for the outside world to intrude. Sometimes a nasal drone from a wooden pipe signalled the arrival of the snake charmer. At first Tommy would watch from a safe distance but gradually he would creep closer, fascinated by the spectacled hoods of a pair of cobras swaying to the mournful music. Sometimes of an evening Tommy overheard snippets of news from the world outside when his parents and friends drank their whisky and soda on the veranda of an evening.

'So Mankad's googlies did for Compton and Bedser. Only four years since independence and they've won their first test match against us. No wonder they're getting so uppity.'

'More than uppity, Frank. Forgotten what happened to Fitzpatrick? Forcing him into the furnace while it was running at max heat. Men he had worked with for years, just because he wouldn't up their pay enough.'

'But I was talking to Mrs. Sinha about it and she said that Frank would be safe. The CP has him down as a good boss....'

'I wouldn't trust those CP wallahs as far as I could throw them, Blanche...'

For a moment Tommy saw the glaring flames and felt the scorching heat of a furnace, as hands pushed the helpless victim to his death, before his mother sent him on his way to the little room and Laloo the bearer's bedtime stories.

Laloo was not just a bearer, more an all-purpose fixer who could serve at dinner, mind children, mend a leaking roof, deal with a dog suspected of rabies, drive the car. It was the last role he particularly relished. In his khaki uniform, moustache recently trimmed, he cut an elegant figure photographed next to the shiny new Sunbeam Talbot. One for the family album.

That evening he was master storyteller and began: 'Tommy Baba, Sita was the most beautiful woman in the world and when she marry Rama they very happy, but demon king Ravana was jealous, kidnap her and took to Lanka. Then Hanuman, the monkey god, help Rama to find his beloved and conquer Ravana in big battle with his bow and arrow. At Divali, Tommy Baba, we light oil lamps to show Rama and Sita safe way home from Lanka. But Divali also is time of Goddess Kali. She is the goddess of death, she is all black with a big red tongue; she has belt of human heads and dress of human arms. She is all powerful mother, can destroy and create. At

Kali Puja, we sacrifice goat, buffalo, all living things and set off crackers, burn fires to frighten evil spirits...'

And Tommy drifted off to sleep dreaming of epic battles and joyful reunions while always there lurked a figure in the background seeming to merge with the darkness of night.

One morning during Divali, Tommy awoke feeling vaguely troubled by something he was looking forward to and something he was dreading. Then he remembered. The day before he had looked up at the peepal as usual and noticed a flash of yellow and black in the crown of the tree. A golden oriole, tempted by the luscious fruit, had been snared by a piece of thread which had entangled its feet with one of the branches. A desperate flutter of wings and then it would hang still. Tommy watched, transfixed by the plight of the bird, his inability to help almost unbearable as he could feel its reserves of energy being used up. Seeing Tommy's distress, Laloo tried to climb the tree and set it free, but the height and flimsy branches proved too difficult, despite the boy pleading, 'Please, please, make him go higher.'

'But Tommy the branch might break and Laloo might fall and....'

'And what then Mummy?'

The bird was doomed and Tommy could not bring himself to watch any longer that day. The next morning he looked up once more. There it hung, stiff, swaying in the breeze like a garish puppet, shrunk in size as if its flesh had been consumed by the burning sun. The heart-shaped leaves of the Peepal were moving, as usual.

But today was the start of Kali Puja, something he had been longing for, when Hindus (and fellow travellers) celebrated the terrifying Goddess Kali by setting off fireworks – the spectacular flaming fountains and starbursts at the Victoria Memorial but also the little bombs that could be thrown at the porch wall or the Atashi wheels spraying orange sparks in a circle of fire.

Back in September he had been rummaging in his mother's desk drawers one wet monsoon day and had seen some fireworks held over from the previous year. Covered in shiny bronze paper, they were a treasure horde, especially a large Atashi wheel, like a rare ammonite hidden in a bed of sedimentary rock. For weeks he had been circling around the desk, the front of the drawer a wall fencing off the forbidden, dangerous but desirable. But now, the first day of Kali Puja, he could no longer resist. While his mother was giving her morning instructions to the cook in the kitchen, he opened the drawer, grabbed a few fireworks, making sure he had the Atashi wheel, ran outside to Chabila and the others, and held aloft the precious prize in triumph.

The boys could not wait for darkness, and on the wide concrete base in front of the garage they set up a crude support for the Atashi wheel. Chabila, who was older and partial to an occasional 'bidi', had a box of matches and lit the touch paper. The group moved a little distance away as the firework began to sputter. Placed flat on the ground rather than fixed to a wall, the flames shot out horizontally and showered the little group in sparks, causing great hilarity, as the boys ran around the circle of fire. Suddenly there was a burning under his chin, and Tommy felt a searing pain in his neck, cheek and ears as his bandage caught fire. The flames shot up, several inches, a foot. He smelt the burning cotton wool and tore at the bandage, but scorched by fire his fingers fumbled impotently. The other boys ran around Tommy, eyes wide open, yelling. Why wouldn't they help? Were they afraid?

Did they not want to? What did the yelling mean? His thoughts became confused. Now he could smell burning flesh. Then he was vaguely aware of something entering the gates. A moment later strong hands were tearing off the bandages.

'It's okay Tommy Baba, Laloo is here.' And Laloo carried him, shouting out in agony, up to his mother. 'Don't cry Tommy, it's all right, Kali no get you this time!'

Rushed to hospital, the burns were cleansed and shots of penicillin given. Infection was prevented but Tommy's glands swelled up.

'He looks like a corpulent Indian god,' said his father.

'What, with those pretty blue eyes?' said his mother.

There was concern he might not be able to breathe. After a week, though, his face and neck were back to normal and Tommy was venturing into the garden once more for a game of marbles with Chabila and the others, who sheepishly welcomed him back. A different type of bandage round his neck. Laloo also sported bandages on his hands, and, for a week, he basked in the gratitude of his employers. If he had not driven through the gates in the Sunbeam at that moment Tommy would have been doomed. But soon the bandages came off and Laloo took up the usual round of duties once more.

News of Laloo's death came through a telephone call one morning the week before Christmas. Tommy had been pestering his mother for some kites and, to humour her convalescing son, Laloo was sent to buy some from the market. On his return he needed to pass between two stationary vans before crossing the street to the Sunbeam. As he did so a lorry, out of control, hit the back of one of the vans shunting them together and crushing Laloo.

He died an hour later of massive internal bleeding. The next day a policeman in crisp white shirt and trousers, carrying Laloo's clothes, his few personal items, and four brightly coloured kites which had survived the accident undamaged, came to the house and explained what had happened.

'Very unfortunate sir, a simple mistake, and a life taken away, so needlessly.'

The officer insisted on laying out the khaki uniform to show the stains where Laloo had been hit by the vans, and placed the kites next to it. For a moment Tommy imagined the familiar moustache and smile, the strong arms filling out the uniform. But then it became a lifeless khaki husk once more. Another, similar, image flashed in his mind. For a moment he seemed to grasp a pattern in the events, but then it passed.

'Can I go and play in the garden with Chabila now mummy?' he said, and took the four kites to show off his latest treasure to his friends.

That night there was no bedtime story. Tommy was restless and his sleep was broken by vivid dreams. In them he felt the lure of the gilded fireworks once more, the elation of setting light to the Atashi wheel. He saw the circle of fire, relived the agony at his neck, Chabila yelling, his own helpless fumbling at the bandage, and Laloo at last saying, 'Kali no get you.' But what was that figure on the edge of the circle, its black limbs glinting against the darkness? He forced himself to walk towards the figure though his feet felt weighed down by lead. Step after step, like wading through quicksand. Closer, he could see four black arms, a bloody kukri, a decapitated head, the obscene red tongue, the belt of human arms. It stood astride a prostrate human form, laughing exultantly.

Despite his terror Tommy was being driven towards the demon god by some power. Now, just a few feet away, he made himself peer closely into its face.

'No! No! No!'

His shrieks brought his mother to the bed and soon he was being comforted in her arms.

'Don't be afraid, sweetheart, it was just a silly nightmare'.

'Yes,' he sobbed, 'horrible, a knife all bloody, like the head, so many arms trying to grab me...' But he could not bring himself to describe the face. The blue eyes.

In the new year, another bearer was taken on, but Tommy missed the old stories of Rama, Sita and Hanuman, the monkey god. For a few years, at Christmas, Laloo's heroism would be remembered. Further into the future, grandchildren and greatgrandchildren would sometimes ask about the scars on Tommy Chisholm's neck. They would be shown the fading photograph of the bearer in his khaki uniform next to the Sunbeam Talbot. Laloo had become a family icon.

Heroes

'Thronging through the cloud rift, whose are they the faces?

Faint revealed yet sure divined, the famous ones of old...'

A catch in his voice, a tear in his eye, Bateson marvelled at the power of the old school song. Accountant, farmer, businessman stood a little straighter, gazes fixed on the banners flanking the stage or the freshly painted coat of arms above. As he looked around the memorial hall, half recognizing features blurred by time, he noted marks of age, the thickened waists, complexions liver-spotted or too florid, the colour leached from grey and white hair. What had brought them back to this Shropshire market town after nearly fifty years, back to the marble memorial plaques, the gilded eagle supporting the school bible and, up against the north wall, the organist in his box, pulling stops, treading pedals, nodding time to lagging voices?

The service had followed a tour of the present buildings and estate. Mixed now, the school had provided his group with two fifth form girls as guides. Puppies straining on a leash, the girls were eager to show off the school: new arts block, indoor pool, sports hall; bright, stylish buildings brimming with equipment. They enthused about sporting successes, the latest sixth form musical, their recent trip to the UN Youth Assembly, a visit from a media celebrity. They were weekly boarders, their talk punctuated with 'mum' and 'dad' and family pet.

Bateson remembered his own school routine of class room, sports field, dormitory, Sundays marked by tolling bells and the long crocodile file to church; the two or three months of separation from family, the rare home visit and shy, faltering talk with mother or sister; long wet weekends indoor that suddenly erupted in the goading of a boy afflicted by stammer or 'girlie' voice.

'... Was it for mere fool's play, make-believe and mumming,

So we battled it like men, not boy-like sulked or whined...'

Well, had he made the grade, had he stiffened lip and stifled tears? In his first winter at the school and new to frozen sheets, a harsher, alien code, he was caught one night rolling marbles on a ledge by his bed. The dorm prefect was determined to use the ultimate sanction, like a terrorist fondling the latest Kalashnikov, a beating by the Beak. A sleepless night, an untouched breakfast, the long walk through corridors to the housemaster's inner sanctum. As he trudged, with the early sunlight streaming through passage windows, he could hear the boyish chatter from the dining hall. Finally he entered the study. The Beak made him kneel, took out a leather-bound bible from a drawer and recited a passage. He asked the boy to bend down and whipped his buttocks six times with a rattan cane. Helpless before the searing pain, Bateson couldn't stifle moans or hold back tears. Humiliated, he turned to his punisher, and was surprised to see the Beak's hands shaking, lips white and drawn, his whole body quivering. A hoarse 'Get out boy'.

Then in his sixteenth year, there suddenly appeared Mr. Wild, biology teacher for the Science Sixth, and known of course as Oscar, Ossie. Tailored suits, black hair smoothed down in a perfect parting. No narrow scientist, but lover of Gropius and the Bauhaus, the French Nouvelle Vague, Resnais, Truffaut. Bateson remembered a biology lesson.

Pipe held at a jaunty angle, Ossie enters the lab to a buzz of expectation. With a toreador's swirl his gown is removed and a rich odour of tobacco mingled with cinnamon wafts over the front rows. The briar is placed in its mahogany stand.

'Today we are going to study how food travels through the human gut,' he begins, 'and I intend to use you boys to mark the stages on this perilous journey. Bateson, you can be the food, may I suggest a morsel of escalope de veau, and Titchmarsh you the enzyme pepsin.' He then allocates oesophagus, stomach, upper and lower duodenum, appendix, colon. 'And you, Usher-Smith, odious slug, you can be the rectum for forgetting your exercise book last week.' The boys are lined up in the appropriate shape and digestion begins. 'Now, Titchmarsh you've got to rough up Bateson a bit to show the action of the enzyme... Come on Bateson, get on with it, or do you need a dose of salts?' Bateson makes his way through the digestive system, being pulverised by a series of punches, and gets as far as Usher-Smith. 'And now, Bateson, a really convincing exit please!' Ossie turns to the blackboard with his box of chalks. The thirty two feet of the human gut are represented by a series of curlicues, the hepatic portal vein tricked out in royal blue, the salivary gland in pink, green for the pancreas, and an elegant little flourish for the appendix. It is a masterpiece.

Sporting ambitions fell away amongst Bateson and his group. On afternoons they searched the local ponds with drag nets for dragon fly larvae, fearful carnivores, for the exotic *ranatra linearis*. Back in the lab they marvelled at the feathery gilled axolotl nosing amongst the pebbles in the aquarium, suspended in its larval stage without the iodine needed to complete metamorphosis. They cherished favourite anecdotes: a class being shown Ossie's latest Chagall print.

'But Sir, I've never seen a donkey flying over roof tops.'
'Well, boy, don't you wish you had?'

The ending of the school anthem shook Bateson out of his reverie and back into the present. They processed out of the hall and into the science laboratory for a talk on the school's volunteer work by the head girl. Recently redesigned, the lab's white melamine work surfaces and dazzling array of glass jars, troughs, dissecting trays, polished black microscopes created an impression of sterile perfection. Impossible to imagine the room as it had been – dusty leaded windows, steeply raked stalls in dark varnished wood, the blackened brass of Bunsen burners, faded rubber hoses.

Or almost impossible. Suddenly, a long suppressed memory of a biology class: Ossie is dissecting a pig's heart, identifying aorta, ventricles and mitral valves, the pulmonary connection. Attention wandering for a moment, Bateson idly surveys the graffiti on his bench top for any updated erotica. Suddenly he sees the ugly, misspelt, carved letters, 'OSSIE IS A SECRET FETICHIST ARE YOU IN THE BLACK BOOK?'

From that moment the horizons of Bateson's world seemed to close in again. In the days that followed details began to emerge. Bewick, the school's top twitcher and beetler, with his own key and free range of the labs, had noticed a large, black, leather bound book in one of the cupboard drawers used by Ossie. He became curious and on a quiet afternoon took his opportunity.

'Some very compromising photographs,' he solemnly pronounced.

This was enough for adolescent minds. Lurid imaginings about 'the Black Book' were discussed, Ossie represented on desk and toilet wall in increasingly grotesque pornographic poses. A low murmur began to accompany him as he swept up the aisle at morning assemblies. In the fevered atmosphere fascination was turning into hatred and Ossie was beginning to notice this. His dress lost its gloss and neatness, his hair its uniform black and his usual poise began to falter as he stumbled over words in lessons.

The crisis was signalled by the ringing of the bell early one February morning, which meant that the whole school was required to attend assembly. It signified something serious, an expulsion or at least a public caning. Someone caught smoking in the old rifle range? Or sneaking a pint at The Bricklayers? Behind the cricket pavilion with Charlotte Brown? The entire teaching staff processed through the hall and onto the stage. At least not quite entire – Ossie was missing. The headmaster swept in and took up position behind the gilded eagle, like any captain at the prow of his ship, facing perilous waters.

'I have something of the utmost seriousness to announce...,' he began.

Ossie had entered the lab early that morning to find the room filled with gas. Someone had left all the taps on. Fortunately he did not have his usual lit pipe in his mouth or the consequences would have been fatal. As it was, the gas had taken its toll of the live specimens. Through the glass of the observation hive, the massed corpses of bees could be seen, and, in their cage, the white mice, pathetic in their last sleep, the little white buck teeth clearly visible. The axolotl floated on the water's surface, fated never to reach adulthood.

Bateson felt that something had to be done. The school was moving towards catastrophe. Should he step back, before the inexorable march of events? He made his decision. Stealing the lab key from Bewick, he got up early one morning and made his way through the deserted corridors to Ossie's office. He opened the drawer. The Black Book was there. He stuffed it inside his jacket, returned the key unseen, and went in to breakfast.

Filled with guilt and apprehension, he awaited the consequences of his act. Nothing happened. Ossie looked white and drawn for a few days but gradually regained his composure. With no immediate quarry in sight the pack lost interest in Ossie and his book and turned their attention to...

Bateson couldn't quite remember, as they filed out of the science laboratory after an impressive talk by the head girl on the school's outreach programme. There was to be one last event. A formal dinner, to be held not at the school but at the town's one restaurant. Seven o'clock found him seated at his table. Within earshot, there was, on his left, the wife of the current P.E. master and on his right an old classmate. Opposite there was Pressland, whose well-tailored white dinner jacket and floppy velvet bow-tie stood out amongst the hired suits around him. Pressland had been one of those schoolboy entrepreneurs. With his camera and order book, he was often on the fringes of parties, school trips and prize days, taking photographs which he would sell for a few shillings. After school he spent some years as a jobbing photojournalist. His big break came with a telephoto shot of a society hostess being goosed by a minor royal at a summer house party. Together with its caption 'Could these be the fingers of a future king?' it was the iconic image of that year. He became a founder of the modern day paparazzi, and recently there had been a lavishly produced book of his collected works, *Camera Indiscreta*. He was appearing on chat shows and giving interviews to magazines.

The dinner began quietly with polite, safe questions about health and hotel accommodation, but as the wine flowed the volume began to rise. Members of the old rugby team had managed to seat themselves together and were beginning to try out a few of the old songs. Bateson was having difficulty following the conversations. On his left the wife describing her son's gap year in Nepal and on his right the classmate describing the long-drawn out breakdown of his marriage. Now and then Pressland's piercing voice would intervene with snippets about his celebrity life style:

'Jonathan and I had a good laugh about the slapper. He can be very indiscreet off camera you know...'

Suddenly Bateson snapped. The wine, the noise, Pressland, it was all too much, and, in his loudest voice, 'I have an indiscretion of my own to confess,' he said. Puzzled faces, a pause. 'I stole the Black Book!' Silence around the table as the implications sank in. Then Pressland began, all media speak now fallen away.

'From what I've heard about the book, Bateson, it's your duty to take it to the authorities.'

'It was just photos of knees,' Bateson replied, 'taken from odd angles, the date neatly noted, and for some reason the weather conditions too. The boys were always dressed in their outdoor kit, shorts and windcheaters, and clearly knew nothing about it.'

'But these were vulnerable boys who have had their privacy invaded!'

'Bloody hypocrisy! You've spent your whole career violating the privacy of vulnerable people.'

'You don't get it, old man. It was almost always adults in my case and besides it was public interest, you know. It's your duty to expose Ossie's book so that other victims of that swine will have the courage to speak out.'

'He was a lovely person. He made a lot of lives a lot richer. Do you want to destroy him in his old age?'

'That's not the point. These cases have to be brought into the light so that all the old culture of secret abuse can be eradicated from our society. There's a good story here and I'm going to file it tomorrow. I've got plenty of witnesses to what you've said.'

The wife and classmate nodded vigorously. Furious, Bateson got up and walked out, followed by surprised looks from the rugby table.

Back at his hotel, he tossed and turned all night, unable to sleep. He had brought the Black Book with him, intending to share an amusing hour with some of his closest friends if the opportunity arose. But now, on the bedside table next to Gideon's bible, the Black Book confronted him, an accusation and a dilemma. It broke down to three options. He could keep the book, in which case he would become the story, the man who colluded with abusers, his face on every front page (Pressland had been busy with his digital SLR earlier that day), police at his door. His table companions would back up Pressland's story. Or, he could take it to the nearest police station early next morning, explain that conscience had given him the courage to confront an offender from the past, and he would become hero. He got up next morning feeling raw, pestered by lines from 'Heroes', the old school song. He had made his decision. Before breakfast, he made his way in the early morning sunlight through empty streets. The police station was just the other side of the Severn bridge. He hesitated for a moment at the top of the bridge, pulled out the Black Book and threw it into the river. Deny its existence, the third option. Let Pressland do his worst.

Going through a gorge at this point, the current was very powerful and quickly tore the book open, releasing the photographs. He could see the occasional figure before it disappeared into the depths. Was that Bickerstaff? Or perhaps Jarvis Junior?

Acknowledgements

I am deeply grateful to my wife, without whose robust encouragement these stories would never have seen publication. I would also like to thank family and friends for useful feedback on early versions – and help with translations.

I am indebted to Carole Angier, *Jean Rhys*, and Lilian Pizzichini, *The Blue Hour, a Portrait of Jean Rhys*, for information on Jean Rhys. My wife and I will always be grateful for the afternoon tea we were treated to by Willis and Elisabeth Feast at Booton Rectory in the winter of 1965.

Also by the same author

A Reader's Guide to Michael Ondaatje's
The English Patient, Bloomsbury.
ISBN 0-8264-5243-4

Language and the Quest for Political and
Social Identity in the African Novel
Woeli Publishing Accra, University of Michigan Press.
ISBN 978-9964978358